COUNTRY STORM

KING CREEK COWBOYS

CHEYENNE MCCRAY

Copyright © 2024 by Cheyenne McCray LLC

All rights reserved.

No part of this book may be reproduced in any form or by any electronic or mechanical means, including information storage and retrieval systems, without written permission from the author, except for the use of brief quotations in a book review.

This is a work of fiction. Names, characters, places, and incidents are either the product of the author's imagination or used fictitiously. Any resemblance to actual business establishments, events, locales, or persons, living or dead, is entirely coincidental.

CHAPTER 1

Frigid air conditioning chilled Rae Fox's face as she guided her car toward King Creek. Arizona sunshine glared down from a clear blue sky as a mirage wavered ahead, like water running across the road. It was the first of June, and they were well into summer.

What she wouldn't give for a long drink of iced tea and a swim in her backyard pool.

Ex-backyard pool. She swallowed. Was that life gone forever?

Instead of a comfortable home, was a prison cell to be her new residence?

Weight pressed down on her chest and she struggled to breathe. One night and her life had changed so drastically, she was afraid it would never be normal again.

Her family had been such a support to her through all of this. Rae's sister, Carrie, had been with her every step of the way. Carrie still lived in Coyote Lake City with her husband and kids. Rae wished she could see her sister and her nieces more often.

Her cousin, Marlee, had encouraged her to move to King Creek to get away from the barrage from the news media that would get worse during the trial, and the constant bullying on social media. Rae had moved in with Marlee temporarily and had only been in King Creek for a week, but already it was a breath of fresh air being in this small community.

Ahead a stopped car took up the right side of the two-lane road. The driver side door had been left open as a slight figure walked to the front of the vehicle.

Rae frowned as she slowed her sportscar and came to a full stop. It was her first day on the job at Mickey's Bar and Grill, and she couldn't afford to be late. She'd been lucky that Mickey had just opened a restaurant attached to his bar, so he'd been hiring.

She blew out her breath as she tapped her fingers on the steering wheel. The figure moved slowly and then stared down.

Something had to be blocking the road. Rae climbed out of her car and shut the door. Heat blasted her like a furnace as she strode toward the little Nissan.

"Hi," Rae called out, but the person didn't look at her. "Is everything okay?"

As Rae gained ground, she realized it was an elderly woman who stood in front of the car.

The woman looked at Rae, her lined features strained. "I don't know what to do." Her voice trembled, whether from age or emotion or both.

Rae's heart rate picked up as she jogged the rest of the way, thankful the country highway was otherwise deserted.

When she rounded the car and the woman, she saw a mixed-breed brown dog stretched out on the road, its fur matted with blood. Her stomach dropped at the sight of the poor wounded creature.

Her heart pounded faster as she knelt beside the animal that tried to raise its head. It sank back down, as if it had been too much effort.

"He came out of nowhere," the woman said. "I don't know what to do," she repeated.

Rae glanced up into the woman's tear-stained face. "Don't worry, I'll take him to a vet. Do you know one in the area?"

The woman blinked, as if it hadn't occurred to her. She must have been in too much shock at hitting the poor dog.

"Doc McLeod." The woman pointed in the direction Rae had been traveling. "Two miles up, you take a right on Thunderbird Trail. His practice is in the second building on the right."

"Got it." Rae stood and droplets of sweat rolled between her breasts and down her back. "I'm going to grab a blanket from my trunk. Can you stay with him?"

"Of course." The woman nodded.

Rae hurried to her little car, popped the trunk, and grabbed an old blanket she kept there. She hurried back to the woman and the dog before kneeling and putting the blanket on the road beside the dog. She hesitated. She'd heard that dogs in pain could bite a person trying to help them.

There was nothing for it—she had to do whatever it took to save the animal. The dog whimpered but didn't snap at her as she lifted him just enough to get him onto the blanket. Blood coated her hands and forearms as she moved him.

"You're a dear to take care of him," the woman said.

"I'd better hurry." Rae scooped up the medium-sized dog and stood. "You take care," she added to the woman.

The woman held up an old-style flip phone in a shaking hand. "I'll call Doc McLeod and let him know you're on the way."

"Thank you," Rae said.

"Bless you, child," the woman called after her.

The dog whined as she carried him to the passenger side of her small car. "You're going to be okay, boy. The vet is going to fix you right up."

She settled him on the floorboard, tucked the blanket around him, and shut the door. She rushed to the driver's side and climbed in.

Rae carefully drove around the elderly woman's car, then

pressed down on the pedal, driving faster than she had been before stopping to help. Rae had to get the dog to the vet in time to save him.

As she drove, she talked to the dog, trying to soothe him the best she could. She tried not to think of the fact she was late for work and wouldn't be able to make it in on time for her first day. By the time she finished and went home for a shower, at least the first half of her shift would be over. She hoped Mickey wouldn't fire her.

The important thing right now was that she had to get this little guy to the vet.

In just short of two miles, Rae located Thunderbird Trail and took a right. She prayed she'd find the vet there. The woman had said she would call Doc McLeod, but that didn't mean he'd be in.

She parked in front of a small pale-yellow building with a hanging sign that read, "Superstition Veterinary Clinic, Dr. B. McLeod."

"Hold on, boy." She looked down at the dog who lay limp but with his eyes open. "I can't get you and the door, so I'm going to see if I can get someone to hold the door open."

She climbed out and hurried the few steps to the clinic entrance. She opened the door just enough to look in. A tall man in a white lab coat stood just inside the door—the vet no doubt.

"I have a dog that was hit by a car." She rushed to get the words out.

The big bear of a man had already been moving toward her the moment he noticed her, covered in blood.

"Maude called a few moments ago," the vet said as he hurried by, straight for her red sportscar. "This your car?"

"Yes," she said, and he opened the vehicle.

In an easy movement, the big man gently scooped the animal into his arms, shut the car door, and turned toward the clinic. Just a few steps and he was headed away. "Thanks for bringing him in," he said in a low drawl as he strode into the clinic.

Rae re-parked her car in one of the parking spaces, grabbed her hobo-style handbag, used her key fob to lock the door, and hurried into the clinic.

A vet tech in purple scrubs said to Rae, "I'll be with you shortly," before she left the room.

Rae needed to wash off the blood that had dried on her hands and forearms. Nothing could be done for her T-shirt. She spotted a restroom sign across the room, through an archway, and made her way to it.

She scrubbed off the blood with antibacterial soap and dried herself with paper towels. When she finished, she returned to the waiting room. She wanted to make sure the dog would be okay, so she intended to wait for news. She fished her cell phone out of her purse and hit redial for the last number she'd called. Now that the dog was with the vet, she needed to contact Mickey.

"Mickey's Bar and Grill," came a deep voice that she recognized as the owner.

"Mickey, this is Rae." She swallowed. "I'm sorry, but I'm going to be late."

"This is your first day," the powerful man said. "I hope you have a good reason."

"An elderly woman hit a dog on the highway." Rae tried not to rush her words. "I helped her and brought the dog to Doc McLeod."

"In that case, being late is understandable," Mickey said. "When can you be here?"

"I got blood on me and my clothes, so I need to run home to shower and put on a clean T-shirt and jeans." She wrapped her arm around her belly. "I can still make it for the second half of my shift."

"That's fine," Mickey said. "We're short-staffed for a Friday, so I appreciate you coming in as soon as you are able to."

"Thanks, Mickey," she said before disconnecting the call.

She let out a slow breath. From what she knew of the man

from her interview and their subsequent phone conversations, he was a good guy, so she'd thought he would be understanding. She was glad she hadn't been wrong.

Her thoughts turned to the dog and she hoped he would be okay. The vet had looked like a man with a big heart, and she felt confident he would do anything to save the canine's life.

Now that she had a chance to work everything through her mind, the vet was one good-looking man. Light-brown hair with a slight wave and hazel eyes. She'd bet he had plenty of return business with female pet owners coming to see the sexy vet.

Rae groaned and swiped hair from her face. She had no idea why her mind had just gone there.

She needed to leave so that she could get to work, but she wanted to find out if the dog would be okay.

Dogs had always held special meaning to her, likely from her father's shared love for the four-legged creatures. She'd grown up running around his pet supply store and when she was a teenager helped him hold dog training and behavior modification classes.

That had all ended when her dad passed away of complications from a routine surgery. Her world had shattered when he died. It had been fifteen years since his passing, but she still missed him so much.

She'd always thought she'd be in the same business as her dad, but life happened, and she had ended up as a real estate agent for the largest Realtor in Coyote Lake City. Of course, she'd lost her job in the mess her life had become. So, she'd sold her home and fled to this small town to stay with her cousin, hoping she could get lost when she wasn't having to travel three hours each way for the trial. It wouldn't be long before she'd have to face that drive.

"Ma'am?" A female voice drew Rae's attention toward the archway, where the vet tech now stood, holding a chart.

Rae gripped the strap of her handbag tightly in one fist. "Is he okay?"

At the tech's nod, a wave of relief flooded Rae.

"Dr. McLeod will be out shortly to give you the full status."

"Thank you." Rae knew she had to leave, but she wanted full confirmation from the vet. For the first time, she wondered about the dog's owner. Did they even know their pet was missing to begin with? They would be relieved to hear he would make it.

The vet walked through the archway, and when his hazel-green eyes met hers, Rae's skin tingled head to toe. Dear God, the man was H.O.T., *hot*.

He was so tall, and she was so short, it felt like she had to keep looking up, up, up. He stepped forward and held out his hand. "I didn't get a chance to introduce myself. I'm Dr. McLeod. I've never seen you around these parts."

"I'm Rae Fox." She had a hard time catching her breath. "I just moved here. I'm staying with my cousin, Marlee."

"Marlee Fox?" he asked.

She nodded. "I imagine you know her since this is such a small town."

"I sure do." He slid his hands into the pockets of his lab coat. "I see her cats." He smiled. "Welcome to King Creek," he said.

"Thank you." She gripped her hands together. "How is the dog?"

"Our little friend is going to be just fine," Dr. McLeod said. "He has lacerations, bruising, and leg fractures. He's young and he'll heal up well."

"Thank goodness." Rae relaxed. "His owners will be glad he's going to make it."

"I've never seen him in my practice, and he doesn't have a collar or tags," the vet said. "I'm the only vet in the area, so I see most of the pets in our town. By his size and how thin he is, I think he might be a stray."

Rae frowned. "I hope not. He deserves a loving family."

"If we don't locate an existing owner, we'll try to find him a good home."

"That's a relief." She smiled at the vet. "Thank you, Dr. McLeod."

He returned her smile. "You have a good day, Ms. Fox."

She felt a strange urge to continue their conversation, despite needing to hurry so that she could get to work. "Call me Rae, please."

He gave a slow nod. "You can call me Bear."

The name fit the big man who looked like a huggable Teddy bear. "Thanks, Bear." She stepped back, feeling suddenly nervous and shy. "I'm late for work. Maybe I'll see you around."

"In this small town," he said, "You probably will."

Rae backed up, having a hard time taking her eyes off Bear. She ran smack up against the front door and banged the back of her head. Heat flushed her cheeks. "Bye," she threw out before turning and fleeing his practice.

BEAR WATCHED the pretty redhead leave. She had a sexy, curvy figure and a smile that could light the whole town at night. He didn't remember ever having such a strong, instant attraction to a woman, at least not like the one he'd had when he'd taken her hand in his. Damn, but she had him thinking of moonlit nights on sandy beaches and fruity drinks with little umbrellas.

If he'd had the guts, he would have asked Rae if she'd like to meet him someplace for a drink. He could have offered to buy her something cool for helping save the dog's life.

Of course, he hadn't. His brothers would have given him a hard time for missing out on the opportunity. He just wasn't as good with women as they were.

He faced his tech, Marie. "It looks like our last appointment is late."

Marie flopped in the office manager's chair behind the computer monitor. She squinted at the screen. "Jan has Mrs. Clawson and Butch down for an appointment that was supposed to start fifteen minutes ago." She looked at Bear. "I'll give Mrs. Clawson a call."

"I bet you miss Jan right about now," he said.

Marie rolled her eyes. "She'd better get her butt back in the office soon. She's not allowed to go on vacation again *ever*."

Bear grinned. "I'm gonna check in on the little guy and see how he's doing."

Marie picked up the office phone's receiver. "I'll let you know if I get ahold of Mrs. Clawson."

He gave a nod and strode back to the bank of kennels. He reached the young dog's spot and smiled when he saw the name on the small chalk sign, *Arthur*. Marie always gave human names to pets that were brought in with no tags.

Arthur lay motionless, still under sedation. His chest rose and fell in a deep, even rhythm. "The lady who brought you in is gorgeous," Bear said to the sleeping dog. "Seems like a real sweetheart, too. Maybe I'll even see her around town."

He couldn't help thinking of all of that soft skin that he'd love to touch, and long red hair that would feel silky running through his fingers. He'd bet her head would rest nicely against his chest if they danced and her body would mold perfectly to his. The red shade of her hair was unusual, and he didn't think it was natural. It was cute, but it made him wonder what her natural hair color was.

What was her story? Where had she come from? What brought her to King Creek? Was she just here for a short time to visit with Marlee, or did Rae plan on staying a good long while?

Marie's footsteps came from the hallway and he looked over his shoulder.

"Mrs. Clawson forgot about Butch's appointment." Marie changed from speaking in her Hispanic accent to a southern drawl that was a perfect imitation of Abilene Clawson's voice, "She's right sorry to miss her appointment and hoped you wouldn't mind if she reschedules." Marie dropped the drawl. "She's set for Wednesday morning."

Bear did his best to not laugh. "Looks like our Friday is ending early." He inclined his head in the direction of the wounded dog. "I'll take Arthur to the ranch so I can keep an eye on him over the weekend."

"Sounds good, Doc." Marie pulled her long, dark ponytail over her shoulder and slid the elastic band off and over her hand to rest on her wrist. She fluffed out her hair. "I'm glad to get out of here early. Candy set me up on a blind date for tonight, so with not-so-high hopes for this latest guy, I'm going to head home and soak in a long hot bath and hope he cancels."

Bear grinned. "Where's he from?"

"Chandler." Marie sighed. "City boy."

"You'll have a good time." Bear added in a teasing tone, "Even if his neighborhood's probably the size of King Creek."

"Unfortunately, it probably is." Marie shook her head. "I'll see you Monday."

"You have a good weekend, and I hope your date is fun."

"Me, too." She smiled and grabbed her purse out of her desk drawer. "Go find that cute redhead who brought Arthur in. You could use a night out."

Bear mumbled a response as heat crawled up his neck. It was bad enough his brothers teased him, but now his tech, too?

Marie left with a little wave and Bear turned back to the sleeping dog. "I kinda hope I do run into that pretty lady," he said.

Even if he wouldn't know what to say if he did.

It was one thing being the town vet and working with people professionally. It was a whole 'nother thing getting on a personal level with folks he didn't know—namely women.

Bear closed up shop and grabbed Arthur's portable kennel to take with him. He loaded it up in the back seat of his king cab and headed home.

By the time he reached his ranch, Arthur was stirring. Bear

carried the kennel into his home, parked it in the big kitchen, beside the refrigerator.

"Hi, Bear," screeched Mervin the macaw, a rescue also named by Marie. "Mervin missed Bear."

Bear grinned. "I know you're hungry, Mervin. Just hold your horses."

"Mervin hungry, Mervin hungry."

Maggie and Katie, a pair of ragdoll cats, showed up and eyed Arthur suspiciously. The girls normally wound around Bear's feet when he got home, but tonight they were concerned who the stranger was.

He reached down and rubbed the cats behind their ears. "Arthur is a very nice dog, so everything's just fine."

Both cats mewled. They were used to him bringing home animals who needed extra care, and this one was safely in a kennel, so their concern faded.

Bear crouched in front of Arthur. "We'll get you up and around and healed up, boy. Meanwhile, I'm gonna see what I can do to find your family, if you've got one. If you don't, we'll make sure you get a good home."

Arthur thumped his tail on the kennel mat but didn't otherwise move. Likely, he wasn't feeling too well after being hit by the car. That was enough to ruin anyone's day.

Bear got Misty's old water bowl, rinsed it out, and filled it with fresh water. Misty, a Border collie that had been with him for over a decade, had passed away a couple of months ago.

He bent on one knee in front of Arthur's kennel with the bowl of water, opened the door, and placed the bowl in the corner to his right. The dog thumped his long tail a few times, as if in thanks.

Arthur was a young lab-retriever mix that probably had some Australian shepherd mixed in. If the dog had been any older and well fed, he probably would've been too heavy for Rae to pick up.

Bear left the house for the barn and took care of his

menagerie before dinner. He fed the horses and his few head of cattle, treated the rabbits to pellets and lettuce from the barn refrigerator, and gave the ducks and chickens their evening chow. When he came back into the house, he fed Mervin, then returned to Arthur's kennel.

"You're a beautiful boy," Bear said. "Play your cards right, and I just might know someone who'll be happy to take you in."

Arthur thumped his tail and raised his head.

"Thirsty?" Bear gave a nod toward the water bowl. "Go on now and have a drink. It's gonna hurt, so be careful."

Arthur tried to get up and stopped with a whimper. He tried again and again, and finally got his head over the bowl. He took a few laps, then sank down again.

"Wore you out." Bear opened the door, reached in, and stroked Arthur's head.

The dog thumped his tail once again.

Bear closed the door, got out Maggie's and Katie's dinner and put it in their bowls, and the pair happily started eating.

His phone rang. He reached into his back pocket, pulled his phone out and saw it was his brother, Colt.

"Hey, bro." Bear rose to his feet. "What's up?"

"Put on your best hat and boots," Colt said. "We're going out tonight and finding you a woman."

Bear shook his head, but he couldn't help a smile. Colt was the exact opposite of Bear in many ways, and that included when it came to women. Colt was forward and could find a date easily where Bear had a hard time asking women out.

"I—" Bear started, but Colt cut him off.

"Don't even try to come up with an excuse. Meet me at Mickey's at eight. We'll shoot some pool and find someone cute for you to cuddle up to."

Bear wanted to laugh, but the first thing that came to his mind was Rae Fox. Cute and definitely someone he'd like to cuddle up to. Maybe he'd just happen to run into her tonight. Well, a guy could dream.

"All right," Bear said. "See you there."

"On time," Colt said.

"I always am." Bear disconnected the call and looked at Mervin. "Guess I'm going out tonight."

"Going out tonight," Mervin shrieked. "Going out."

CHAPTER 2

"Got it." Rae gave a single nod to Mickey as he finished giving her instructions to start her shift. They stood behind the bar and she'd demonstrated she could make drinks well and handle his simple point of sale, POS, system.

"Go get 'em, young lady." Mickey, a large, muscular man who looked like he was pushing sixty, moved away from the bar. "I've got to take care of some work. Jane will help you in the bar area if you have any questions or get overwhelmed. If all else fails, you can come and get me."

"I'll be fine." She smiled at Mickey and hoped she was right. The last time she'd tended bar was close to ten years ago, when she worked part time at a small place in Coyote Lake City while working full time as an office manager for a realty company. Once she got her real estate license, she had quit working at the bar and concentrated on her new career.

"Like climbing back on a bicycle," she told herself.

Rae faced the bar and smiled at the only patron sitting on one of the stools, a man who'd been introduced as Jim.

He gave her a nod and she moved closer to him. "What can I

get you, Jim?"

Jim raised his beer bottle. "Gimme another."

"Coming right up." She reached into a cooler, grabbed a bottle, and used an opener to pop the cap before setting the bottle in front of him.

"When did you move to town?" Jim looked like he might be in his sixties, with skin tanned like leather from hours in the sun and crinkles around his eyes.

Rae shrugged. "A couple of weeks ago." Before he could ask a follow-up question, she asked one of her own. "What do you do?"

"Ranchin'." Jim shifted on his stool. "I'm foreman for Colt McLeod on the Bar M."

"Is he related to Doc McLeod?" She hadn't been able to stop thinking about the sexy vet, no matter how hard she'd tried.

"Yes'm." Jim tipped back his bottle and took a long swallow before thumping it back on the bar top. "You met Bear?"

Rae gave a little smile. "Earlier today. I took an injured dog to his practice."

"He's a good ranch vet," Jim said emphatically. "Best there is. Good man, too." Clearly, Jim thought highly of Bear.

Two couples walked through the doorway and headed for a table for four. Looked like business was picking up and it was about time for the evening to get going.

"Doc McLeod seemed nice," Rae said, which was a complete understatement. He was a big, huggable, teddy bear. She'd never had the kind of reaction to a man like she'd had to Bear when she'd met him. He'd seemed friendly and approachable, and she'd frozen and tripped up all over herself like a silly schoolgirl. Maybe if she met him again, she'd get to know him better.

Damn it. She had no business thinking anything like that. She bit the inside of her cheek, using the pain to remind herself that her life was far too complicated right now to get involved with any man. What if things went badly, and she lost the case?

Her heart pounded in her throat. She didn't want to think that way. She couldn't imagine what would become of her.

Not that he'd be interested in her, anyway. He probably had a sweetheart, or even a wife. Maybe kids, too.

The thought was strangely depressing.

She sighed.

Jane came from the direction of the table for four, reached the bar, and leaned over it. "Two rum and cokes, an amaretto sour, and a Long Island iced tea."

"Coming up," Rae said. She smiled at Jim before turning and making the drinks. Those were simple enough. She just hoped she could handle anything more complicated. After all, it had been a *long* time since she'd tended bar.

Like getting back on a bicycle, she reminded herself.

The night grew increasingly busy, and the other bartender who was supposed to have come in was late. Between filling Jane's orders from the surrounding tables, making drinks for patrons sitting on stools around the bar, and filling the waitress's orders from the new grill part of the establishment, Rae didn't know if she was coming or going. She had just given a pair of women margaritas on the rocks when she noticed two men climbing onto stools at the end of the bar.

Rae moved closer to them and almost tripped over her own feet when she saw that one of the men was Dr. Bear McLeod.

Next to him sat a man with amber eyes. He had light brown hair and looked enough like Bear that they had to be brothers.

Her cheeks warmed when Bear's hazel eyes met hers and he smiled. She felt shy again, something that had never been a problem for her before. What was wrong with her?

"Hi, Doc." She smiled and tried not to stare too long into his eyes.

His smile made her feel all wiggly and squishy inside. What was she now—a gummy bear?

"Howdy, Rae. I told you to call me Bear." His rich tone was

enough to make her shiver inside. "I told you we'd run into each other again."

For the life of her, she couldn't look away from him. "That you did, Bear." Lord almighty he was so good looking.

"I'm Colt." The other man's voice cut into the connection between her and Bear. She forced herself to look at the other man, when she just wanted to focus on Bear.

Colt was grinning at her, with a look that said he'd seen exactly what she was thinking when she was staring at Bear. "Bear is my little brother."

There was nothing little about Bear McLeod.

Her cheeks burned. She cleared her throat and held out her hand. "I'm Rae."

He took it in a firm grip. "A pleasure to meet you, Rae."

"Rae brought in an injured dog this afternoon." Bear drew their attention. "Thanks to her, Arthur is doing just fine."

"His name is Arthur?" Rae asked. "You found his family?"

"No on his family," Bear said. "Marie, my tech, named him Arthur for the time being."

"He looked like he's probably a sweet dog." She wanted to lose herself in Bear's eyes.

"Bartender." A whistle came from the other end of the bar.

She turned to the man and raised her hand in acknowledgment. She glanced back to Bear and Colt. "What will you two have?"

"Go on and take care of Bill Porter." Bear nodded in the direction of the man who'd just called out to her. "We'll order when you've got a moment."

"Thanks." She smiled at Bear and hurried to the other end of the bar.

The whole way she could feel Bear's gaze on her. Or was it? What was going on with her that she *wanted* him to be watching her? Wasn't it just this morning that she was wishing people would *stop* watching her when she went out in public?

Her face had been plastered all over the newspapers all the way to Phoenix, and she'd hoped King Creek would be small enough that no one would have heard about her and what had happened. And now she was hoping she had a man's attention?

She reached the man Bear had referred to as Bill and she asked him for his drink order.

He looked her up and down in a way she did not appreciate—like he was imagining her naked. This time her cheeks burned for a different reason.

"You're new here," Bill said with a grin he'd clearly meant to be sexy, which turned her off entirely.

"Yep." She answered him with the one-word to hopefully cut him short. "What can I get you?"

Bill leaned forward, his arms on the bar top, getting into her personal space. "What time do you get off work?"

Rae took a step back. "I've got a lot of people at this bar needing to order. What do you want?"

He didn't seem put off in the least. "I see what I want right in front of me."

"Then I guess you're not thirsty." She mustered up a polite smile. "I hear someone calling out for me. Let me know if you decide to order."

She turned away and moved to a pair of women who'd climbed onto the stools a few down from Bill.

After she took their orders, she filled them, refusing to look in Bill's direction. He didn't call out or whistle again, so she assumed that he'd moved on. At least she hoped he had.

When she'd finished making drinks for the two women, she finally glanced in Bill's direction. Not there. She blew out her breath. *Good.*

She returned to Bear and Colt. She felt off balance when she was near Bear, like she couldn't steady herself around him. She made herself look at Colt first, then Bear. "Sorry it took me a bit to get back to you."

"Just ignore Bill." Bear appeared concerned and like he wanted to comfort her. "He shouldn't be acting like that, but he's harmless."

"Bear's right." Colt chimed in. "Bill's an ass at times, but that's about as far as it goes with him."

Rae smiled at both of them. "I'm used to it. You get that a lot as a female bartender."

Bear looked uncomfortable. "No one should treat you or any other lady with anything but respect."

"Thanks." She wanted to put her hand over Bear's to show her appreciation, and to feel the warmth and strength of him. Instead, she looked at Colt, too. "I'm sorry, but I'm afraid someone else is going to need me, so what will you two have?"

Both men ordered domestic dark beers on tap as well as two orders of onion rings. "I'll be right back with your drinks, and I'll put your order in." Rae turned away, regretfully not being able to sit there and talk with Bear and stare into his eyes.

For goodness sake, she had to stop this.

She put the order for the onion rings on a tray for Jane, then filled two ice-cold mugs from the freezer beneath the bar.

She handed Bear and Colt their beers, but before she had a moment to say anything else, Jane gave her another order. Jane picked up the food tab Rae had set in the tray and headed for the kitchen.

Rae moved from patron to patron, making drinks and taking bar food orders that she delivered as they arrived. Her feet were killing her, but more than anything, she was so aware of Bear that she had to work hard to focus on her job and not on him.

She had to get her head where it belonged and away from Bear McLeod.

"She's got it for you bad," Colt said to Bear as they watched Rae tend bar. "She keeps looking your way when she thinks you're not looking."

Bear shook his head. "A woman like that is not interested in a guy like me."

"Hell, why not?" Colt blew out his breath. "You're too damned shy for your own good."

Bear shrugged. "I'm not as comfortable with women as you are."

"You're a McLeod." Colt looked honestly puzzled. "None of us has a problem with talking to women but you. You must get it from Dad."

Bear laughed. "If I'm being compared to Dad, I'll take it as a compliment."

Colt grinned. "Ordinarily, being compared to him is a good thing. In this case, remember that if Mom hadn't asked Dad out, none of us would be here."

"True." Bear couldn't help a smile. "Maybe I am a little too much like him in this regard."

Colt slapped him on the shoulder. "There you go. Now get up some courage and ask her out, bro."

Bear took a deep breath. Colt probably had it right. He just needed to ask Rae for her number, or maybe if she'd meet up with him at Heidi's Coffee Shop. That shouldn't be too hard, should it?

As busy as she was, he wondered if he'd ever have a chance to ask her.

Bear sat and worked up his courage to ask her as he watched her. She smiled at the men and women sitting at the bar as she took their orders and when she delivered them.

He wondered what it would be like to hold her in his arms. He'd bet she'd be soft and warm, a perfect fit.

"Bear." Colt's voice jerked his concentration away from Rae. When he faced Colt, his brother had a grin a mile wide. "If you don't ask her out, I will. She's awfully cute."

The thought of Colt dating Rae made Bear's gut clench. The

last thing on earth he wanted to do was watch his brother with Rae.

"Keep your hands to yourself," he found himself saying to Colt. "I'll ask her when she's got time."

Colt picked up his beer. "You'd better. She's too sexy to let slip away."

Bear tried not to frown. It wasn't like him to be jealous of anyone, and that included his brothers. But when it came to Rae, he had a real hard time keeping his emotions in check.

What was it about her?

She was beautiful, that much was for certain. It was clear she had a big heart, too—she'd brought the dog to him when she'd helped Maude earlier today. He'd seen it in her eyes, just how relieved she was that Arthur would be okay. You couldn't fake that kind of caring.

He'd always had a good read on people, which was one reason why he kept his distance from some women. He didn't mean to be judgmental, but he always got a feeling that staying away from certain people was the right decision for him.

Of course, Jennifer Mayfair had been the exception to that rule. He'd read her all wrong. She'd asked him out on a date, and they'd started seeing each other regularly. She was a brunette with an English accent, which had seemed sexy at the time. He'd thought things had been going well for the three months they'd been dating.

Until he caught her having sex with another man.

Bear stared at his beer, tapping on the glass with his thumbnail. He'd left his wallet at her house, and when he went to pick it up the next day, her front door had been wide open. He'd called to her, but no answer. That fact had given him some cause for concern. Had she hurt herself? What if she needed help?

He'd heard something from the direction of her bedroom and had walked down the long hallway to her open bedroom door.

When he saw her on the bed, another man between her

thighs, he'd gone cold. She'd seen him and her eyes had widened, and she'd looked frantic, like she knew she'd made a huge mistake.

He'd just turned around and left, a cold, cold feeling in his gut.

That had been around four months ago or so, and thoughts of it still made him sick. Jennifer had begged and pleaded for him to take her back, but he'd continually put her off until she finally got the message.

Bear had an easy nature, but he'd only let someone cross him once. After that, he'd be polite, but that was as far as it would go. He might be what his brothers called a softy, but he wasn't a fool.

A nudge to his ribs had him cutting his gaze to Colt. "What's up, little brother?"

Bear shrugged and took the focus away from himself by asking, "How's Alice?"

Colt groaned. "Hell if I know. One day she was all over me and the next she didn't return my call and I haven't seen her around." He shook his head. "I'm not going to chase her down, so if I hear from her, I hear from her."

Bear gave a slow nod. He'd never had a good feeling about Alice, but he hadn't said anything to Colt. That wasn't his place. All he could do was hope he was wrong and hope for the best for his brother.

Rae approached them and Bear straightened on his stool. Colt jabbed him in the ribs again with his elbow, a clear indication that now was the time to make his move.

Bear smiled at Rae. "You're keeping mighty busy."

Rae pushed a strand of hair that had fallen out of her ponytail away from her face. "It's slowing down a little. But I shouldn't jinx myself like that."

He looked around the bar. He hadn't noticed the crowd had thinned. How late was it? He glanced at his watch, surprised to see it was after ten.

"It's about time for the late rush," Bear said. "Do you have anyone to relieve you?"

Rae nodded. "Patty just got here, so after I take care of you two, I'm going on break."

Patty had been with Mickey since the man had opened the place, some twenty years or so earlier. Bear had been just a kid.

Colt elbowed him again and he shot his gaze to his brother. Colt mouthed, "Ask her."

Heat flushed over him as he looked back at Rae. "It's hot in here and I could use some fresh air. Mind if I join you on your break?"

Rae hesitated, then smiled. "Sure, Bear." She glanced at the neon Budweiser clock above the bar. "Five minutes from now should do it."

"I'll be ready, Rae," Bear said.

She looked at Colt, then Bear. "Need another cold one?"

Colt shook his head and raised his glass. "Still sucking this one down."

"I'm good," Bear said.

"Hold on, Bear, and I'll see if Patty can cover for me now." She smiled and turned away.

Damn, but he liked the way she said his name.

"Good job." Colt slapped his shoulder. "Fast thinking on your feet."

Bear rubbed his ribs. "With a little reminder."

Colt laughed. "Any time."

Five minutes later, Rae waved to him and he left his stool to join her at the far end of the bar. She seemed so shy and sweet as he looked down at her. He hadn't realized just how petite she was until that moment. He must have been too focused on her face back at the clinic.

"Come on." She inclined her head toward the kitchen. "We can go out back."

He walked at her side, keeping his strides short so she could keep up with him.

Rae and Bear headed through the kitchen where Manny was cooking up pretty good bar food. They continued to the back door. He pushed it open and held the door until Rae had walked through.

Outside was cooler. The desert usually cooled down significantly at night, enough that it was a relief after a hot day.

Bear shoved his hands in his front pockets as he stood beside Rae, and she bit her lower lip before meeting his gaze. "It's been a heck of a busy first day."

Bear smiled. "I didn't know it was your first day working for Mickey."

She nodded. "I was late because of Arthur, but thankfully Mickey was understanding and let me miss the first part of my shift."

"He's a good man," Bear said. "I see his dog, Hamburger, at my clinic."

"Hamburger?" Rae laughed. "That's his dog's name?"

Bear grinned. "Hammy is a rescue—a teenager at the adoption center had started calling him by that name. It stuck and Mickey figured Hamburger was as good a name as any."

"I like Mickey." A light breeze teased the loose hair that had fallen from her ponytail. "I could tell he would be a good person to work for."

"Where did you come from?" Bear asked.

Rae's expression shifted. Only slightly, but it made him wonder why.

"Coyote Lake City." Her throat visibly worked as she swallowed. "I needed a new start and I decided a small town would be a better fit for me. Marlee has been bugging me to move in with her forever."

It seemed like there might be more behind what she'd told

him, but he'd wait 'til he got to know her better—at least he hoped he would.

Before he could ask her another question, she said, "What about you?" She tipped her head to the side. "What's your story?"

He shrugged. "Born and raised around here. I've got a big family and we're all over this valley."

It was now or never. He cleared his throat. "I was wondering if you'd like to meet me for coffee at Heidi's tomorrow. Say, maybe ten in the morning?"

Rae smiled. "I'd love to." Her expression shifted and he had the impression she wanted to take back her acceptance. But then she blew out her breath and straightened her shoulders. "I need to do laundry in the morning, so ten is good with me."

What was it he kept seeing in her eyes? Something like a haunted look. Had he been reading her all wrong and she wasn't who he'd thought she was? He mentally shook his head. No, he was certain he knew the kind of woman she was.

She was running from something, though, and he'd find out what it was sooner or later.

Their gazes connected in a way that seemed to lock them into place. He couldn't move. He wanted to kiss her, to hold her, to make her feel like everything in the world was good and whole.

The door opened behind them and they lost the connection they'd just shared. Jane came through the doorway and she held open the door. "I need a break, Rae. Can you fill in for Patty so she can cover me?"

"Sure." Rae nodded. "I'll take care of it now."

Jane just seemed to notice Bear. "Hey, Doc."

"Hi, Jane," he replied with a nod.

Rae cast a smile at him, and he followed her back into the kitchen and then the bar. He joined Colt while Rae took her place behind the bar.

"You ask her out?" Colt asked the moment Bear slid onto his stool.

Bear gave a nod. "Coffee at Heidi's tomorrow morning."

"It's not dinner and dancing, but it's a good start." Colt folded his arms and leaned forward on the bar. "You're scoring better than me tonight."

Bear picked up his drink. "What went on while I was gone?"

Colt shook his head and laughed. "Alice came in. She's with some out-of-towner. You can tell by the way he dresses that he's not from around here. City slicker if I ever saw one."

Bear looked around the bar. After a moment, he spotted Alice with a guy that definitely did not look like he was from King Creek. Polo shirt, slacks, loafers, and a big gold watch. Yeah, definitely not from around here.

"You're better off without her." Bear turned to Colt and said what he'd told himself he wouldn't say. "I never had a good feeling about Alice. There are a lot of great women out there, and you deserve someone who'll be good to you."

Colt studied him for a long moment. "You're right." He sighed. "One day I'll meet her. Not giving up until I do."

Bear turned his attention back to Rae just as she placed three fruity drinks in front of a trio of women.

She glanced at him and smiled before moving to the next patron at the bar.

Bear took another swig of his beer. He was more than looking forward to tomorrow.

CHAPTER 3

*R*ae felt reenergized after her break outside with Bear. It didn't feel like she'd been on her feet for hours.

Every now and then she would glance in Bear's direction. Not too long after their talk outside, he'd left his seat and she hadn't seen him again. Colt had stayed and talked with people around him, but no one sat on the stool Bear had previously occupied.

She'd been disappointed he'd left, but at least she'd see him tomorrow.

A couple of hours later Bear returned, and she'd realized she was smiling again.

Rae had tried not to look in his direction all night, but she'd failed in that regard, repeatedly.

During one of the moments she forced herself not to glance at him, she grabbed a bar towel and wiped down the bar top. She shouldn't feel so excited about a coffee date when starting a relationship was a bad idea. Especially since she'd be moving to Albuquerque once the trial was over.

She wiped away a spill on the bar top. Marlee kept encouraging her to stay in King Creek, but it wasn't far enough away.

The thought of moving sobered her some, but she pushed it

away. Meeting Bear was a bright spot in the gray her world had become since she'd killed a man.

Her throat tightened and she couldn't get rid of the feelings of doubt and pain that encased her again. She refused to look in Bear's direction, in case he saw how she felt written all over her face.

Why couldn't she enjoy something as simple as a relationship?

For one, her plans all along had been to flee to another state when the trial was over. And two, she didn't need to burden anyone else with what she was going through—Bear certainly didn't deserve that. There was an even bigger reason. What if she was convicted and she went to jail?

Then there was a big fat reason: she'd killed someone. What man would want to be around a woman who had taken someone's life?

Steve sure hadn't. He'd dumped her not long after it had happened and had gone so far as to imply that she had encouraged the man that led up to the "incident."

Tears threatened behind her eyes. She faced away from the bar and stared at the shelves of liquor bottles around a large mirror as she swallowed hard.

What she needed was to go forward with her plans and start a new life, get away from the haters and online bullies. She'd closed down all of her social media accounts, but there were still the newspapers and constant recognition that had driven her away from her home and her career. Who wanted to buy a house from a murderer?

She held her hand to her belly. It hadn't been murder—it had been self-defense. Everything would be fine, as long as the jury didn't find her guilty.

Yes, a new start was everything.

"Bartender." A man's voice jerked her out of her thoughts, and she whirled to face the person currently leering at her.

Bill. She couldn't deal with him if he was going to treat her like he had earlier. She couldn't—wouldn't—put up with it.

She forced a smile and walked to the end of the bar where he stood.

His gaze dropped to her breasts. "Hey, sugar."

"Up here."

He raised his head, his eyes meeting hers. "Huh?"

"My eyes are right here." She pointed to them and spoke as calmly as possible. "I don't see with my breasts."

He gave her a grin that was meant to be sexy. "Who says?"

She wanted to punch him. She wasn't in an emotionally stable place to deal with this crap. Of course, she should have thought of that before she decided to take a job tending bar.

"What can I get you, Bill?" It amazed her how she managed to keep calm as out of control as her emotions were right now. "Like I told you before, other people are here for drinks, too."

He leaned one forearm on the bar. "What do you say to pizza at Louie's tomorrow night, just you and me."

"Even if I wasn't working tomorrow night, I would say no." Restrained anger edged her voice. "As a matter of fact, you could be the last man on earth and I'd still tell you to go have pizza by yourself."

Bill laughed. "We'll see."

Could anyone believe this guy?

"Last chance." Clenching her jaw made it hard to get the words out. "Do you want to order or not?"

"Gimme a Bud." He grinned at her. "Add an order of fries with the works."

She gave a single nod and turned away to take care of his order.

When she took him his beer, she refused to meet his gaze and slammed the Budweiser down in front of him. It was a wonder she didn't slosh it over the edge of the bar top and onto his lap.

After taking care of a couple who'd ordered a Crown and

Coke and an import, she finally glanced at Bear. He was watching her with something like concern. Clearly, he'd seen she was upset, even though she'd tried not to show it. She wasn't surprised he'd be intuitive like that.

She moved to him and did her best to smile at him and Colt. "Anything I can get you two?"

Bear shook his head. "I've had enough for tonight."

"Same here." Colt checked the clock over the bar. "Looks like it's about time for the bar to close."

Surprised, she glanced at the clock, too. "I didn't realize it was so late." She'd missed it if Jane or Patty had shouted last call. Relief flowed through her. Thank goodness this day would soon be over.

When she looked back at Bear, he was studying her. "Are you okay, Rae?"

She took a deep breath then exhaled. "Just tired. It's been a long day."

"If you need me to have a word with Bill, let me know," Bear said quietly. "I might be able to talk some sense into him."

Rae wanted to laugh. "You can't talk sense into a man like Bill. They don't know how to shut it off."

"I can have a conversation with him," Bear said.

Rae shook her head. "It's fine. If it comes down to it, I'll take care of him."

The last man who'd harassed her in a bar had ended up dead, so maybe those weren't the best words to use.

She tried again. "I'll be fine, Bear."

He gave a slow nod. "Just the same, I'll walk you to your car when you get off work."

She sighed and offered him a smile. "Okay." She glanced at the clock. "But it'll be fifteen to thirty minutes after the bar closes before I can get out of here."

"I can wait," he said.

"Thank you." Rae left to take care of other patrons. Since the bar was closing soon, she would be cleaning up rather than making drinks.

Rae stopped wiping down the bar when she heard Patty calling her name. Rae hadn't had much of a chance to talk to Patty because they'd been going non-stop since the woman arrived.

She turned and faced Patty, whose mascara dotted her skin under her eyes like punctuation marks. Her lipstick was crooked, and her skin weathered like old parchment. She looked as if she'd smoked for decades and had a hard life.

"Been a while since you've tended bar, hasn't it," Patty said like a statement, not a question. "It shows."

Rae's skin prickled at the way the tall woman looked down at her like she was a beetle she wanted to squish with her fist.

"It's been a few years," Rae said.

Patty snorted. "Looks like it's been longer than that."

Rae's skin burned. She didn't need this belittlement from Patty, but she would have to sit here and take it, regardless. She needed this job.

"Is there something in particular that I need to work on?" Rae asked as calmly as she could.

"Everything." Patty pointed to the bar top. "Get that cleaned up so we can get out of here."

Rae bristled. As far as she knew, she didn't answer to anyone but Mickey. Still, she turned away and started working on spots like she could carve into the wood with the rag.

"You've done great today." Jane stood beside Rae as she set down a stack of tickets. "For a first day, you rocked it." She jerked her thumb over her shoulder in Bill's direction. The man was downing a final swallow of beer. "And you survived that hick."

Rae smiled at the kindness Jane showed her, unlike Patty's treatment. "I appreciate your help with my questions. You made it easier for me." She looked at the almost empty tables. "You're good at your job."

Jane shrugged. "It's nice working for Mickey." She leaned in close and spoke so only Rae could hear. "Don't let Patty get to you. She's like that to everyone."

"Honestly, that's a relief." Rae relaxed her shoulders. "According to her I did a terrible job."

Jane patted her shoulder. "Patty is another one who can't shut it off."

Feeling slightly better, Rae glanced in Bear's direction to see he and Colt no longer sat at the end of the bar. They'd probably gone outside. Maybe Colt was leaving, and Bear had walked him out.

Mickey returned and helped close up the bar.

"I didn't get a chance to check in on you tonight," Mickey said as he helped her put chairs on a table. "But I hear from Jane that you handled everything that came your way. Good job."

She'd seen Patty talking with Mickey, too, and had been afraid the woman would make her look bad. The relief she felt at his praise was like a weight off her shoulders. "Thanks."

"Go on home now." He waved his hand to the door and raised his voice. "Go on now, all of you."

Jane had grabbed her purse from the back room and was now walking through the bar. "You don't have to tell me twice, boss."

Rae hadn't brought a purse, had just stuffed her jeans' pockets with her keys, driver's license, cash, a credit card, and a tube of lipstick.

She said good night to Mickey and gave him a little wave. Patty still stood near the door to the kitchen and the back room. Rae called out to her. "Night, Patty."

Patty gave a nod, a sour look on her face.

"Come on, Rae." Jane gave a nod toward the entrance. "It's been a hell of a night."

"It's been one heck of a day," Rae said.

The cooler evening air brushed her skin as they left the bar and stepped onto the wide porch. Bear stood to her right, his shoulder hitched up against the weathered wood post that helped hold up the roof over the porch.

Her heart thudded a little faster when she saw him. The man was so dang good-looking, from his Stetson all the way to his cowboy boots. Every lickable inch of him was sexy.

When their gazes met, she smiled. "Thanks for waiting, Bear."

Jane stopped at the edge of the porch. "How long have you two known each other?"

Bear looked at his watch. "Nine hours, twenty-nine minutes, and eight seconds."

Jane burst out laughing. "Have a good night, you two." She waved and jogged down the steps to the parking lot.

Rae's cheeks warmed. As much as she'd like to find out what a good night was with Bear, that certainly wasn't happening—at least not tonight, if ever.

"I moved my truck closer to your car." Bear gave a nod in the direction of where she'd parked.

At first, she wondered how he'd known which car was hers, then she remembered he'd seen it when he'd taken Arthur from the passenger side. There probably weren't many little sportscars like hers around King Creek.

They walked side-by-side to her car. Bear stuffed his hands into his front pockets like he wasn't sure what to do with them.

She could think of lots of things.

Inwardly, she groaned. She didn't know what was getting into her. She hadn't even looked at a man twice over the past year, since that awful night.

She breathed in slowly, deeply, then exhaled. Another time, another world.

"How are you doing after your first night on the job?" Bear asked.

She glanced up at him. He was so big and tall he made her feel even more petite than she already was. His hugs would have to be the best thing ever.

"Not bad." She smiled. "I'm tired and looking forward to a good night's sleep." She cocked her head. "How do you think Arthur is doing?"

"I went home and checked on him a couple of hours ago," Bear said. He's doing pretty good, as well as can be expected."

"That's where you went," she said without thinking first.

"So, you noticed?" he said with a grin.

Rae laughed, not minding the warmth in her cheeks. After all, it was dark. "Sort of."

He grinned. "Good enough."

They reached her car and came to a stop beside the driver's side door. "I'm looking forward to tomorrow," he said.

She pulled her keys out of her pocket and smiled at him. "I am, too."

He looked suddenly shy again, and she felt equally shy.

She hit the unlock button on her remote and heard the sound of the door lock disengaging. Before she could reach for the door handle, Bear opened the car door for her.

"Thanks," she said as she got in.

Bear closed the door behind her and waited while she buzzed down the window.

"See you at ten," he said.

Rae smiled. "See you, Bear."

She buzzed up the window, put the car in gear, and headed toward the parking lot exit. She glanced at her rearview mirror and saw him watching her drive away.

The range of emotions she felt was enough to make anyone crazy.

She kept her breathing even and allowed herself to think of Bear. He was so sweet and thoughtful and a gentleman. What a great combination in a man. That and the sexy package he came with was more than enticing.

But not only was her situation bad, she also didn't plan on being here long.

Now, she wished she could. But she had to make a new start, had to get away from a town where people would recognize her and question what she'd done. Even if the jury declared her innocent, the stigma would still be attached to her.

In Albuquerque, she could get her real estate license and start all over, building up a list of clients. She could buy a nice house with a pool and make it her home, even more so than the one she'd sold.

She hated to leave behind her sister and her nieces in Coyote Lake City, but Carrie understood her need to get away and start a new life. The kids would miss her, almost as much as she would miss them. She wouldn't be as close to Marlee, so that wasn't so great, either.

Rae and Carrie's parents had passed away when they were teenagers, which was back when her family lived in Albuquerque. Their dad had owned the pet shop before he died from the surgery complication. Their mom had been a nurse and less than a year later contracted a virus that had killed her.

Rae and Carrie had been devastated and had become even closer, needing each other more than ever when they'd gone to live with their maternal grandmother in Coyote Lake City. Their grandmother had been a cold, hard woman, so the sisters had relied on each other for comfort and to make it in their new home.

Almost fourteen years later, and Rae was facing a trial with the possibility of going to prison. She shuddered. She didn't think she could survive prison.

She glanced at the clock on her dashboard and saw that it was almost one a.m.

When she reached Marlee's cottage-style home in a small neighborhood on the outskirts of King Creek, Rae parked and locked up her car before going through the gate and striding up to the postage stamp-sized porch. She used the key Marlee had given her and unlocked the door. She winced at the loud squeak it made, hoping she hadn't woken her cousin.

Marlee was a few years older than Rae, but they'd become close over the years, getting together as often as they could with the miles separating them.

A light was on by Marlee's chair. Her cousin happened to be in the chair, working on one of her crazy quilts.

Marlee looked up from her quilting. "Hi, Rae."

"What are you doing up so late?" Rae plopped on the chair closest to Marlee. "Aren't you usually in bed by now?"

Her cousin set down her hoop, stretched her arms, and yawned. "Sometimes, when I'm working on a quilt block that I'm really excited about, I can't stop."

Rae craned her neck. "Can I see?"

Marlee passed her the hoop with the portion of the crazy quilt she was working on.

Rae traced her fingers over the embroidered square that consisted of various velvets, brocades, satin, and silk pieces with embroidered seams and lace and crystal embellishments. "It's a work of art." She shook her head in amazement. "I can't imagine putting in the time it would take to do something so incredible."

Marlee smiled. "Thanks."

"Aren't quilts something older ladies do?" Rae smiled and teased her cousin. "You know, things Red Hat ladies work on." She pointed at her cousin. "You, on the other hand, like to dance, jog, play sports, and have a wild time with the girls. Somehow crazy quilting doesn't fit my preconceived notions of a crazy girl like you."

"You just said it," Marlee grinned. "A crazy girl who happens to like crazy quilting because it's just plain crazy."

"Ahhh." Rae laughed. "Now it makes sense."

"Why don't you give it a try while you're here?" Marlee took the hoop that Rae passed back to her. "You might enjoy it like I do."

Rae held up her hands. "I have zero talent for needlework."

"I thought the same thing about myself at first." Marlee smiled. "You don't know if you don't try."

"You never know." Rae pulled her hair back away from her face. "I need to cut my hair so that I look even more different."

"That shade of red probably makes you look different enough." Marlee studied her. "It's such an odd shade, but it does look good on you. Almost as good as your normal blonde."

Rae thought about Bear, and wondered if he liked her hair color, or if he thought it was odd. "I saw Bear McLeod at the bar tonight. He said the dog that lady hit is doing well."

"That's great." Marlee slipped her quilting paraphernalia into a large basket and closed the lid. She focused on Rae. "He's cute, isn't he?"

Rae's face went warm. "Yes."

Marlee's eyes widened. "You like him."

"Of course, I like him." Rae cheeks burned. "He's a nice guy."

Marlee laughed. "If you could only see how red your face is."

Rae groaned and buried her face in her hands. She raised her head. "I screwed up, Marlee."

Her cousin looked puzzled. "In what way?"

"Bear asked me out for coffee in the morning and I said yes."

Marlee brightened. "That's awesome."

Rae shook her head. "No, that's terrible."

Now Marlee looked confused again. "Say what?"

"I shouldn't start a relationship with any man." Rae's throat constricted. "What if I end up going to prison?"

Marlee narrowed her gaze. "You are *not* going to prison. The man followed you to the houseboat and tried to rape you. He even said he was going to kill you for rejecting him at the bar."

Tears threatened behind her eyes. "Haters on social media say I dressed like a slut and a tease and asked for it."

Anger churned across Marlee's normally calm features. "Don't listen to them. That's why you deleted all of your social media accounts. You did, didn't you?"

Rae sighed. "Every last one of them. Even Pinterest."

"Pinterest?" Marlee raised an eyebrow. "I couldn't live without Pinterest."

Rae smiled a little at her cousin's gentle teasing. "Okay, so maybe that was going farther than I needed to. But I got rid of everything."

"I'm glad you took that step." Marlee leaned forward in her chair, her forearms braced on her thighs. "You got away from Coyote Lake City, so you won't be spotted, and you won't see the newspapers."

"And you're kind enough to not watch news while I'm around," Rae said.

Marlee waved away the comment. "That's no hardship. I hate the way the newscasters sensationalize everything. I get my news from a reliable, factual source online. So, I keep up to date without getting bogged down."

Marlee scooted to the edge of her seat. "About Bear McLeod."

"Should I cancel the date?" Rae asked.

Her cousin shook her head. "I don't think so. But if you do pursue a relationship with him, you need to give serious consideration to staying in King Creek and not moving to New Mexico."

Rae churned the thought over in her mind. "I don't know if I can do that. I need a fresh start, Marlee. I need to be able to sell a house without someone recognizing me or my name and saying, 'Hey, aren't you that woman who killed a man?'"

Marlee didn't respond for a moment. "Listen to your heart and take care not to break Bear's in the process."

Rae sighed. "I should cancel the date."

"I didn't say that."

"I did." Rae rubbed her palms on her jeans. "But then, what could it hurt meeting him for coffee? It's not like it's a real date."

"Good." Marlee's smile faltered a little. "You have an appointment with your attorney Monday, don't you?"

Rae's stomach churned at the thought. "In the afternoon. The trial starts in less than three months."

With a soft smile, Marlee said. "Everything is going to be okay, Rae. I know it."

Rae smiled at her sweet cousin. "Thank you."

Marlee got up from her chair. "On a brighter note, I'm glad you're going to get together with Bear. He's a good man, and you can trust him."

Rae stood, too. "I think you're right on both accounts."

"Are you up for jogging with me early in the morning?" Marlee asked. "I'm planning on going a couple of miles outside of town and back."

"Too early for me after a late night." Rae groaned. "My other excuse is I'm dead on my feet after my first day of working at the bar."

"Great excuses—this time." Marlee hugged Rae. "Good night, cousin."

"Sleep well," Rae said and followed Marlee upstairs.

Rae went to the guest room and took off the crazy quilt Marlee had made and set it aside before she sat on the edge of the bed. She took a deep breath and let it out slowly. Tomorrow was a new day and she had a coffee date with Bear. Despite everything, she smiled, looking forward to seeing the big man with the big heart.

CHAPTER 4

*B*ear pulled into a parking spot behind Heidi's coffee shop. He liked to arrive early, and he wasn't surprised he didn't see Rae's little red sportscar.

He entered the coffee shop, the wonderful scent filling his senses. Nothing smelled better in the morning than freshly ground coffee beans. He nodded to the owner, who was behind the counter. "Good morning, Heidi."

"Well hello, Bear." She put a plastic lid onto an iced coffee drink. "Haven't seen you in a while."

He shrugged. "Thought it 'bout time I showed my face in here."

"I agree." Heidi yelled out, "Amy, your caramel latte is up."

Amy Baker wove her way through the tables, and she smiled at Bear. "Morning, Bear," she said in passing.

Bear replied in kind and saw the couch and chairs in the back corner were free. He took a seat in one of the cushioned armchairs, where he had a good view of the front door. He set his Stetson on another armchair to reserve it for Rae.

A few minutes before ten, Rae came through the door. She

was so darn pretty with her long red hair, cute figure, and the beautiful smile she gave him when she spotted him. He tried not to stare at the way her snug blue jeans fit her, or the way her blue T-shirt hugged her, but it was real hard not to look.

He got to his feet and waited for her. It seemed the most natural thing in the world to give her a hug. She returned it and smiled when they separated. He picked up his Stetson and gestured to the chair he'd saved for her.

"How'd you manage to get the best seats in the house?" She plopped down on the cushioned chair. "Ooh, this is comfortable."

He took his own chair and rested his hat on one knee. "Got lucky."

She leaned back and crossed her legs. "This chair is so big it's a wonder my feet reach the floor. I feel like a kid."

Bear chuckled. She sure didn't look like one.

He gave a nod in the direction of the front counter. "What would you like to drink?"

She scrunched her nose as she looked up at the menu. "An iced vanilla latte sounds good."

"You've got it." He left his hat on his chair and worked his way through the tables to the counter.

He ordered Rae's iced latte and a black coffee for himself. "You make the best coffee west of the Mississippi," he told Heidi when she gave him the drinks.

Her eyes twinkled. "And here I thought it was west of the East coast."

He grinned. "My mistake." He dropped a good tip in her tip jar and returned to the corner.

Yeah, it was pretty tough not staring at Rae's body. He hadn't liked how Bill had leered at her, and he was sure she hadn't either. So, staring at anything but her face might make him a hypocrite.

Colt would probably say there was nothing wrong with it, as

long as you weren't an ass and treated the lady with respect. He might have something there.

He handed Rae her latte. "Heidi makes the best coffee. I'm sure it carries over to her other beverages."

Rae accepted it and brought the straw to her mouth as he sat. She lowered the cup with a satisfied expression. "This latte is amazing."

He moved his hat off the chair to the small table between his chair and Rae's. He sat and relaxed, wishing he could stretch out his long legs. "Rested up after your first day on the job?"

"I woke up sore as heck." Rae groaned. "It's been a long time since I've tended bar."

"I'm not surprised. You worked hard last night." He cocked his head. "When was the last time you worked in a bar?"

"It's been almost ten years." She smiled. "Took it as a part-time job to make extra money when I started an entry-level position as an office assistant after college."

"What made you quit the part-time job?" he asked.

"I got my real estate license and began selling properties." She looked a little sad when she said it.

He studied her. "You decided to get out of real estate?"

"Something like that." On a dime she turned the questions onto him. "What's it like growing up in a small town like King Creek?"

"You're raised with everyone knowing everything about you, and you know everything about everyone else." He grinned. "That's how it was when I was young. The town has grown a lot since then, but the gossipy part hasn't changed much."

She shifted in the big chair, bending one knee and putting her ankle under her opposite thigh. He didn't think he'd ever be that flexible.

"I bet you hear all kinds of things, being the town vet," she said.

"I hear my share." He gave a nod. "A lot of it goes in one ear and out the next. I'm not much for gossip."

Rae pushed her fingers through her long hair. "My sister and I got enough of it in high school to last a lifetime."

"How many siblings do you have?"

"Just Carrie." Rae sipped her latte. "She's married and has two toddler girls, so I have a couple of cute rug rat nieces to spoil."

"My oldest brother, Carter, and his wife have twins. My brother, Justin, and his wife have a teenager," Bear said. "It's fun spoiling the kids."

"How many brothers and sisters do you have?" she asked.

"Four brothers and three sisters." He laughed as she widened her eyes. "There are a lot more McLeods around here than that."

"Good grief." She smiled, "My parents and then my grandmother had their hands full with just Carrie and me."

"You grew up in Coyote Lake City?" he asked.

"We lived in Albuquerque until we were teenagers." Rae's eyes softened. "Our parents both passed away the same year. The state sent us to Coyote Lake to live with our grandmother."

"It must have been rough losing your parents so young." Bear couldn't imagine not having his own parents and big family around him. "How is your grandma?"

"She passed away a couple of years ago," Rae said.

"I'm sorry to hear that," he said.

Rae shrugged. "We weren't close. Grandmother kicked me and Carrie out when my sister turned eighteen, which was ten months after I turned nineteen. She was a hard woman."

Bear studied Rae. She'd shrugged like it was a casual thing that she'd said, but he could read her emotions beneath the surface and it was clear it hurt a lot more than she had expressed.

They chatted more about family and King Creek. Rae was evasive about her life before moving here, glossing it over rather than discussing it in detail. Something had happened to hurt her enough to run to his small town, but not enough to leave the state entirely. He supposed she hadn't wanted to go too far from her sister and nieces, and she had her cousin to stay with.

Eventually, she would feel comfortable enough with him to tell him the parts she had left out. At least he hoped she would.

"Ever been horseback riding?" he asked.

"Never." She shook her head. "I've always been afraid I would fall off."

"That's a common feeling people get." Bear watched her for signs of true fear and didn't get the impression she was terrified. More leery than scared. "What would you think about coming to my place to meet my horses? If you feel comfortable enough, we can get you up on a horse and let you ride around the corral. One of these days we can even go for a ride farther on out."

She looked like she was thinking it over.

The way she'd been concerned about Arthur told him she had a soft spot for pets. "I have a menagerie, so if you like animals, I have enough to make you feel at home."

She brightened. "What do you have?"

He listed them off. "Three rabbits, eight chickens, three ducks, two horses, a few head of cattle, two cats, and a macaw named Mervin."

She laughed. "That certainly is a menagerie. Do you have a dog?"

"Not now." He shook his head. "I had a Border collie-lab mix, but Misty passed away a few months ago. I miss that girl. I've been waiting to adopt a rescue and haven't had time to visit a shelter."

"I'd love to see your menagerie." She uncrossed her legs and leaned her forearms on her thighs. "I do love animals."

"This afternoon?" He realized he might be pushing it. "Or tomorrow?"

She appeared thoughtful. "I don't have anything going on later today. Give me your address and I'll see you in a while."

His insides warmed and he felt like a schoolboy, excited about his first date. "Would you like to stay for dinner?" He swallowed. Now that was pushing it. "Least I can do is feed you once you come out all that way."

"Is it that far?" She smiled. "Do I need to pack a lunch for the journey?"

He returned her smile. "Not too bad. Twenty minutes outside town."

"I think I could handle that." She looked suddenly happier, lighter than he'd felt from her before. "I'd love to stay for dinner. Is there anything I can bring?"

"Dessert," he said with a grin.

She looked pleased that he'd suggested something she could bring. In his experience, when people offered, it usually meant they wanted to contribute in some way.

"You've got a sweet tooth, I see," she stated.

"Yep." He nodded. "I love pretty much anything. As a matter of fact, I can't think of anything I don't like."

"I've got some things to take care of before I visit your animals—and you," she said with a smile. "So, I'd better get back to Marlee's. When should I go out there?"

As soon as she could, was his first thought. "How about three?" he said. "That'll give you time to meet all the critters, and if you're up to it, I'll help you get up on one of my horses to get used to it."

"Deal." She started to get to her feet, and he stood and held out his hand before she'd totally risen.

She let him help her up. He liked the feel of her small hand in his and didn't want to let it go.

But he released her and gestured for her to walk ahead of him, out of the coffee shop. He gave a nod to Heidi as he passed her and she smiled and winked at him, as if knowing he was sweet on the woman he was with.

He wondered if it was that obvious, then figured no doubt it was.

When they reached her car and she'd unlocked it, he opened the door for her, and she climbed in, then shut it. She lowered her window as she backed up the car. "See you in a little while, Bear."

He couldn't help a broad smile as she drove away.

Looked like it was going to be the best day he'd had in a long time.

"I can't believe I said yes." Rae paced Marlee's cozy kitchen, gripping an iced tea glass in her hand. "He was so sweet to ask me to his ranch to meet all of his animals. I couldn't help myself."

Marlee kneaded bread dough as she spoke. "Don't feel like you have to tell him everything the first date you have."

"Is that lying by omission?" Rae asked.

Marlee kept kneading. "As long as you don't wait too long to explain to him about the trial and the whole situation, you're fine. You don't need to throw it all at him when you've only just met. Don't overwhelm the poor guy. Wait until the right moment."

"How will I know when it's the right moment?" Rae sighed. "I mean if I let this go any farther."

"Slow down." Marlee put the bread dough into a greased bowl and covered it with a tea towel. "You're getting way ahead of yourself."

"You're right." Rae leaned back against the counter and sipped her tea. "I won't know if there's any real attraction until I get to know him."

"And you'll tell him when it's right," Marlee said.

Rae gave a slow nod. "The trial will be here before I know it. Somehow, I'm going to have to tell him long before then. That's if we're still seeing each other."

"I'm sure you will be." Marlee smiled. "I have a feeling about you two."

Rae drank the rest of her tea, hugged her cousin, and grabbed the pink cake box she'd picked up at the bakery after leaving the coffee shop. She waved to her cousin, headed out to her car, and put the cake box on the passenger seat.

At times she'd felt giddy and excited since seeing Bear this morning, then worried she shouldn't let things go as far as she was, and then smiling and happy about it again. The up and down feelings made her feel like she was on a seesaw.

She drove from Marlee's place onto the highway and in the direction her GPS indicated she should go. Her mind continued to run a mile a minute as she thought about Bear and getting a chance to know him better.

Soon enough, Rae reached the turnoff and drove onto the road that would lead her to Bear's.

The tires on her sportscar bounced on the road as she hit small rocks, and in her rearview mirror, dust roiled up behind her car. It was a wonder her little car hadn't bottomed out on a rut, but so far so good.

She turned left onto a dirt road when she saw the sign for Black Bear Ranch. She couldn't help but think it should be called Honey Bear Ranch because he was such a sweetie. She came up on a sprawling ranch house with a huge barn, a couple of buildings, and corrals. She parked in front of the house, next to a big white truck, and shut off her engine.

Bear walked from around the side of the house and reached her car door. He opened it all the way then offered his hand to help her. She took it and stepped out into the heat. Perspiration instantly dampened her skin.

She'd never been around a man who was a gentleman like Bear. It was sweet the way he opened doors for her and treated her like a lady. It was a refreshing change and made her feel warm inside.

He gave her a big bear hug, appropriate for the big Teddy bear of a man he was.

"I have dessert." She stepped back and started around to the passenger side. He got to the door first and opened it for her. When he saw the pink cake box, he reached inside and brought it out.

"You went to Rachel's." He held the box in one hand while closing the passenger door. "Her baked goods are the best."

"The red velvet cake looked too good to pass up." Rae grabbed her purse and phone, then closed the car door. She dropped her phone into her purse and fell into step beside him as he strode in the direction he'd come from. "I saw the cake in the case through the front window and I was sold."

"I love her red velvet." Bear met her gaze. "Great choice."

His beautiful eyes and sexy smile made her feel like giving a happy sigh. It was ridiculous how this man made her feel, but she had to admit she was enjoying it. No man had made her feel this good, ever.

"I probably should have brought you around to the front door," he said as they walked up to a side door. "Came this way out of habit."

"You don't have to be formal with me," she said. "As a matter of fact, the less formal the better as far as I'm concerned."

He opened the door and stepped aside to let her in. Cool air conditioning met her as she walked into a spacious kitchen with tall oak cabinets, stainless steel appliances, and black granite with green marbling. Every surface was sparkling clean and dust-free. Did he go on a cleaning spree because she was coming over?

Across the kitchen she saw an arcadia door, and through it she caught a glimpse of a lawn and trees.

A small whimper caused her to look down and she saw a kennel with a familiar dog in it.

"Arthur." She got on her knees and rested on her haunches as she studied the bandaged dog. "How are you, boy?"

He thumped his tail and looked at her with his big brown

eyes, in a way that made her want to draw him into her lap and hold him.

"If you were well," Rae said, "I'd give you a big hug." She reached into the kennel and stroked his head. "As a matter-of-fact, when you feel better, I am definitely going to give you lots of hugs."

Arthur looked like he felt better just by her scratching him behind his ears.

Bear crouched down beside her, the cake box no longer in his hands. "He's a good boy and a good patient."

Arthur thumped his tail harder and moved as if trying to get up.

"Rest, boy." Bear gave Arthur an affectionate pat on the head.

"Bear has company," a voice came from Rae's left, and she turned her gaze up to see a macaw in a large cage on a tall pedestal on the other side of the refrigerator. "Pretty lady, pretty lady."

Rae laughed and glanced over her shoulder. "Mervin the macaw?"

"Should have remembered to warn you. Pay no mind to anything he says." Bear gave a sheepish grin. "Except for the pretty lady part."

Rae rose and moved to Mervin's cage. She studied the red bird with green and blue-green feathers. "You're gorgeous, Mervin."

The macaw bobbed his head. "Gorgeous Mervin, Gorgeous Mervin."

Bear came up to stand beside her. "Compliments go to his head."

She looked at Bear. "How did you end up owning a macaw?"

"I adopted him." Bear took the lid off of a nearby clay jar. "Mervin's former owner fell on hard times and couldn't afford to keep all of his animals." Bear brought out a few cashews from the jar. "Give him a couple of these and he'll be your best friend."

She took the cashews. "He won't bite?"

"Mervin is a sweet bird." Bear opened up the cage and let the bird walk up his arm to his shoulder.

The bird nuzzled Bear's ear before he raised his head. "Mervin sweet bird."

Bear gave the macaw a cashew.

Mervin took the nut and ate it. When he finished, he said, "Thank you, Bear."

"You're welcome, Mervin." He gestured to Rae. "Pretty lady is going to give you a nut."

Mervin bobbed his head. "Pretty lady, pretty lady."

Rae fed Mervin the cashews and each time Mervin said, "Thank you, pretty lady."

"You're welcome, Mervin." Rae couldn't help but wonder how many pretty ladies Bear had brought to the ranch. She had a feeling it wouldn't have been many. He definitely wasn't the player type—she'd seen enough of them to know one when she saw one from a mile away.

Bear returned the macaw to his cage, closed the gate and double-latched it.

"You mentioned you have two cats," she said.

"Maggie and Katie will appear when it's time for their dinner," Bear said. "They hide when someone new shows up, but they'll come out for dinner. Sometimes they get curious enough to come out before dinner and investigate."

"I love your kitchen." Rae looked around the large space, noticing the pink cake box now on the huge island. "I have a feeling your whole house is great."

He gave her a little grin. "The critters are what make this a great home."

"I'm looking forward to meeting them all," Rae said with a smile. "Do you have someplace I can set my purse?"

He gestured to an old-fashioned coatrack by the backdoor. "Will that work?"

"Yes, perfect." She hung the strap on a hook.

"Ready to meet the rest of the crew?" he asked.

"Definitely." She crouched next to Arthur's cage again. "See you when we get back."

Arthur thumped his tail.

Rae stood and Bear inclined his head toward the back door. "You can meet Roxie and Angel first."

CHAPTER 5

Bear and Rae left the house for the barn, walking into the heat. They strolled in the direction of the big red structure, the sun beating down on them. A pasture was fenced off to the right of the barn and a corral to the left. Two horses trotted up to the fence, stopping in the shade of several huge Arizona ash trees.

"I owned three horses. Chester, the Quarter horse I'd had since I was a kid, passed away not long after Misty." Bear's shoulder brushed Rae's as they came into the shade.

When they reached the pair in the corral, Bear stood between the horses and stroked their necks. He nodded to the black horse with a diamond on its forehead and a black-spotted white rear-end. "This is Roxie. If you're not familiar with the breed, she's an appaloosa."

"I don't know anything about horses." Rae stopped next to Bear. "She's beautiful." She looked to the other horse, which had a golden coat and a white-blonde mane. "She is just as gorgeous."

"Angel is a palomino." He stepped aside. "Why don't you pet Angel first?"

Rae touched Angel's neck and felt a thrill at being able to

stroke the smooth coat of the palomino. She all but gleamed in the sunlight that flickered through the leaves. "She looks like a river of gold." She glanced at Bear while she touched Angel's mane. "Did you adopt them, too?"

"They came to me in different ways," Bear said. "Angel is from a ranch on the other side of King Creek. The old man passed away and he didn't have any heirs, so he willed her to me. I was her vet, and he wanted her to have a good home."

He rubbed Roxie behind her ears. "Roxie came from a farm where her owners abused her." His face clouded. "When the equine rescue organization got involved, I took her in, and she became a part of the family."

Rae reached out to touch Roxie's forehead as she marveled at the big-hearted man. She'd never known any man as kind and generous as Bear.

"Roxie doesn't shy away," Rae said. "She doesn't act abused."

"She's been with me for six years." Bear smiled at the horse. "I worked with her for a long time before she trusted people. Now she's as gentle and sweet as can be."

He faced Rae. "After you meet the others, would you like to sit on one of them? Maybe take a ride around the corral?"

Rae's pulse quickened. "I think so."

He nodded in the direction of the barn. "The chickens are in a coop on the other side of the barn and the ducks are in a pond in the back. The rabbit hutch is in the barn."

They left the horses and the shade. The sound of chickens came to her as they neared their location and she saw structures beneath more shade trees. She smiled at the sight of the auburn-colored chickens that ran up to the gate when they saw Bear and her approach.

"Are they hungry?" she asked.

"Always." Bear laughed. "They're Rhode Island Reds. They're exuberant, friendly, and inquisitive. They each have different personalities."

"I never realized chickens have personalities," she said.

"They do." As they neared the coop and entered the shade, a couple of the chickens came closer to the gate and made excited-sounding chicken noises. "Rhode Island Reds are also exceptionally talkative." He gestured to the two closest to the gate. "Some more than others."

"I can hear that." She watched the pair. "What are their names?"

He pointed to the smaller of the two. "That's Taco." He gestured to the other. "And that's Pot Pie."

Rae laughed. "Pot Pie? Really?"

Bear flashed her a grin. "My niece, Kaycee, named them." He nodded toward the others. "We also have a Dumpling, BBQ, Buffalo, Kabob, Nugget, and Sesame."

"Too cute." Her grin faltered. "You don't eat them, do you?"

He shook his head. "They're pets and they're good layers."

"How long does it take a chicken to lay an egg?" she asked.

"About twenty-six hours," he said. "I get from five to seven eggs a day."

She widened her eyes. "Don't tell me you eat that many eggs."

"Nope." He smiled. "My mom and dad eat a lot, as do my grandparents, so I give them eggs regularly. Mom picks them up once a week."

"Where did you get all the chickens?" she asked.

"Alice, one of my pet parents wasn't able to care for all her animals anymore, so she asked me if I could find them good homes. I took them in, and they ended up being a part of the family." He gave a little grin. "To be honest, I never thought I'd have a bunch of chickens. But they're a fun bunch."

"They do look like they'd be fun to be around," she said.

"I'll introduce you to the ducks now." They walked around back to a large penned in area with a pond and several shade trees. Three ducks floated on the surface of the pond, quacking louder as they saw Bear and Rae approach.

"The males are Frodo and Bilbo," he said. "The female is Pippa. Frodo and Pippa are mallards, and Bilbo is half-mallard and half-Peking."

"Are they friendly?" she asked.

"They won't sit still to be petted," he said, "but they're more than happy to hang around to be fed."

"I love the quacking sounds they make." Strands of Rae's hair rose in a light breeze. "You mentioned you have cattle."

"None of them are in right now. they're all out to pasture." The breeze stirred the tree leaves, causing light and shadow to filter over Bear's face. "My cattle are the only animals here who aren't adopted or rescues."

"What do you have to show me next?" she asked.

Bear smiled. "You get to meet the rabbits."

"Awesome," she said.

He headed away from the shade of the trees surrounding the duck pond, Rae at his side. He opened the big barn door and smells met her that reminded her of the Mohave County Fair in Kingman. She'd never been in the livestock barns, but she'd walked past them on the couple occasions she'd gone to the fair with her sister and friends.

They left the heat of the day and entered the relatively cool barn, dust motes swirling in the light that shone through as they walked in.

She blinked until her eyes became adjusted to the dimness. Stalls lined one side of the barn, haybales on the other. She followed Bear past an open room that held two saddles and what she guessed were other things for horses.

They moved toward the doors on the front of the barn. On the left was a hutch and she could see rabbits inside.

When they reached the hutch, Rae leaned down and peered through the wire. "Total cuteness."

He pointed to the mostly black rabbit with white patches in one partitioned section of the hutch. "He's Jinx." He moved on to two mostly white rabbits with black spots. "She's Magic and she's Charm. I keep the male separate because I'm not planning on becoming a rabbit breeder."

"They're so adorable." She smiled at Bear. "I've never been around animals like yours before. The only domesticated creatures I've known are dogs, cats, and hamsters."

"Would you like to hold a rabbit?" he asked. "They're pets and used to being handled."

She nodded. "I'd like that."

Bear raised a section of the hutch's roof, reached in, and brought out the smallest female. "Charm is the youngest of the trio."

"Her fur is so soft." She smiled as she took the bunny from Bear. "Rescues?"

"I adopted them from Alice," he said.

After they put Charm back in the hutch, Rae said, "I love your place and all your critters." She tilted her face to look into his eyes. "Thank you for introducing me to them."

"My pleasure." He smiled at her. "Are you ready to try sitting on Angel?"

She swallowed as her belly fluttered. "I think so."

"We'll bring in the horses from the corral," he said as he walked back to the room she'd seen the saddles in. "We'll saddle up Angel in the barn so we can get out of the heat."

The saddles rested on sawhorses, and halters and ropes hung on the walls. Bear took down a couple of halters and returned to her. "We'll bring both girls in. It's getting close to feeding time and I put them up in the evenings."

Rae looked up at him as they stepped into the brilliant sunlight, once again into the furnace-like heat. It got hot in Coyote Lake City, which had tropical and subtropical desert climate, the temperatures sometimes greater than the Phoenix area. After growing up in Albuquerque, it had taken some time to get used to the suffocating heat.

"I'm nervous about getting on a horse," she said as they strode toward the corral.

"We'll take it slow, and if it's too much we can always do it another day," he said. "I want you to feel comfortable about getting on the back of a big animal."

Rae reached into her pocket for a hairband. Bear glanced at her as she pulled her hair up into a ponytail. "You look cute in a ponytail."

She smiled. "Just wait 'til you see me in pigtails."

"Can't wait." He grinned then opened the corral gate, and motioned for Rae to go in. "They're gentle and they won't step on you."

Her stomach made a swooping sensation. From her height, the horses looked *really* big.

She watched as Bear haltered Angel. "Go ahead and take hold of her halter."

Rae tried not to get too nervous as she grasped the nylon halter. "Okay, girl. I hear you and I are going to be good friends."

"There you go," Bear said.

Angel snorted and Rae gripped the halter tighter. She could feel the power of the huge animal through their connection. Angel swatted flies away from her rump with her tail. She shivered her hide, shooing away a fly whenever it landed on her.

After Bear haltered Roxie, he opened the gate. "Walk Angel through, then hold up and we'll join you."

Rae did as he told her. Angel walked slowly at Rae's side as she guided her through, then came to a complete stop when Rae halted. The big horse nuzzled her ponytail, tickling the back of her neck, causing her to laugh.

"So far, so good," she said as Bear and Roxie joined them. "But I think she likes my ponytail."

"I told you it's cute," he said.

They walked the horses, side-by-side to the barn. Bear opened the barn door and he told Rae to go first, and then he brought Roxie through and closed the door behind them.

"First thing we're going to do is brush down the horses. That'll help you to feel more comfortable with her." He patted Roxie's neck. "Stay right here, girl."

Rae swallowed. She was alone with two giant horses. "Don't be ridiculous," she told herself. Bear wouldn't leave her alone with the horses if he didn't feel she'd be one hundred percent safe.

Roxie bumped her head against Angel's neck, and Angel bumped her back.

Bear returned with a couple of brushes. He handed a brush to Rae. "They love being brushed. It's relaxing to both horse and rider."

Rae took the brush he offered, and he demonstrated on Roxie how to use it. She followed his directions with Angel, and he said, "That's great. Keep going."

She fell into a rhythm as she brushed the golden horse and talked to Angel as she progressed. "You are such a good girl, Angel."

Every now and then the horse would snort or bob her head, as if in response. When Rae brushed Angel's rump, the palomino nuzzled the back of her head, causing Rae to laugh.

Bear talked to Roxie as he brushed her, and Rae liked the sound of his voice.

"You're right about this being relaxing," she said as she worked the brush over Angel's flaxen mane. "And I do feel a lot more comfortable with her." She petted the side of the mare's neck. "I think she's more comfortable with me, too."

"You've done a great job." Bear straightened and looked over Angel. "Are you ready to sit on her?"

Rae hesitated then nodded. "Yes."

After putting Roxie in her stall, Bear retrieved a saddle and showed Rae how to properly saddle Angel. "I don't expect you to do it alone, not this time." He cinched the saddle. "It's just good to know how to do it yourself."

Rae focused on his instructions, determined not to get distracted or lose focus. This was important. Angel was a huge animal and Rae had a healthy respect for the physical power this horse had.

"You're not wearing boots," Bear said, "so we won't have you ride. You can sit on Angel's back to get used to her, and I'll lead you around the barn and maybe the corral. I won't have you take control of the reins until the next time, when you're wearing boots."

Assuming there was a next time, Rae thought, but she said, "Okay."

"Ready?" Bear asked.

She nodded and stood on the left side of the horse. Bear linked his fingers together for her to step on and he boosted her into the saddle.

Her stomach swooped as she looked down and saw how far it was to the barn floor. She gripped the pommel tightly. "It's an awful long way down there."

"Better if you don't stare down." Bear rested his palm on her thigh and warmth spread from that touch all the way through her. He seemed oblivious to the feelings she was experiencing, his gaze on her.

She looked away from his lovely hazel eyes and studied her surroundings from her now lofty position. "I feel so high."

"That's because you are." He laughed. "How does it make you feel?"

"Feels kinda awesome." She smiled at him. "I'm a little shaky, but it's cool being this high up."

"I'll lead you around the barn." He snapped a rope onto the mare's halter. "Good with that?"

She took a deep breath and nodded. "Ready."

Bear made a clicking sound with his tongue and Rae's heart

lurched as Angel stepped forward, matching his strides. She clung to the saddle pommel for dear life, as if she was going to fall the very long way to the barn's dirt floor.

"How are you?" Bear looked up at her, clearly intent on making sure she was okay.

"Scared spitless." She managed a smile. "But give me a moment and I think I'll be fine."

Bear kept walking with Angel. "You're doing great."

They circled the inside of the huge barn a few times. Rae relaxed as they rounded the area and found she enjoyed being on the back of such a majestic creature.

Bear said, "Whoa, Angel." The horse immediately stopped with Bear, who patted the mare's neck. "Good girl."

He met Rae's gaze. "You're looking good in the saddle, Rae. Ready for a trip or so around the corral?"

"Yes." She nodded. "Let's do it."

He grinned. "We'll make a horsewoman of you yet."

She smiled and waited as Bear opened the barn door. He led her through as she gripped the pommel. She was glad he hadn't given her the reins. She didn't think she was ready for that just yet.

After Bear closed the barn door, he guided Angel out to the corral. Rae felt every movement of the big animal, yet her gait was smooth and didn't jar her. She went from feeling nervous to experiencing a kind of exhilaration she'd never felt before.

He brought the palomino to a stop and opened the corral gate, took Angel and Rae through, and closed the gate behind them.

Bear stood beside Angel and stroked her elegant neck as he looked up at Rae. "How are you doing?"

Rae smiled. "Great."

"I'm glad you're enjoying your first ride." Bear smiled in return and rested his hand on her thigh, like it was the most natural thing in the world. He didn't seem to notice how the heat of his hand brought on the burn in her cheeks, which had nothing to do with the late afternoon sunshine pressing down on them.

"Ready?" he asked.

She nodded. "Ready."

He released her thigh and she could breathe again. He led Angel around the corral and Rae found herself drawn to Bear's backside. His western hat covered his head, so she couldn't see the wave of his hair. But she did notice how his T-shirt fit the expanse of his shoulders, his large biceps flexing as he gripped Angel's rope.

And O.M.G. but the way his Wrangler jeans hugged his butt was enough to make any woman drool.

Bear looked over his shoulder and smiled. She hoped he didn't notice her face, which had to be red from being caught staring at his backside. If he had noticed her staring, or the redness of her cheeks, he didn't show it in his expression.

He engaged Rae in conversation as she and Angel walked around the corral with him beside them. She had a feeling he was trying to keep her from being too nervous, and it was working.

"Great job." He again rested his hand on her thigh, as if he'd done that for years. "Like I said, I don't feel comfortable letting you do much more than sit in the saddle until you're wearing boots."

"I'll see if I can borrow a pair from Marlee for next time," Rae said.

"Next time it is." He looked pleased, and she had a feeling it was because she'd more or less said she'd be seeing him again, that their new relationship wouldn't end here.

She barely resisted shutting her eyes and shaking her head, as if that might reset her brain.

CHAPTER 6

Bear penned up his small herd of cattle when they came in. Rae helped him feed all of the animals before they headed to the house for dinner.

He had never enjoyed a woman's company the way he had Rae's. She'd been so curious about his animals, asking questions and paying attention to what he shared with her. She'd even ridden Angel, clearly conquering her fear.

"I'm glad it's cooling down." Rae looked at the early evening sky as she walked at his side toward the house. "What's for dinner?"

She tipped her head to meet his gaze as he responded. "I thought we'd throw a couple steaks on the grill, and veggies, as well."

"Sounds wonderful." Her smile caused his gut to tighten. Damn, she was beautiful.

She waited as he opened the back door, then walked past him. She knelt in front of Arthur's kennel the moment she was inside. "How are you doing, Arthur?"

Bear shut the door behind him as the dog raised his head and looked at Rae with his big brown eyes and he thumped his tail. She continued to speak to him in a sweet voice that made Bear smile.

She rose and moved to Mervin's cage. "How are you, Mervin?"

"Mervin hungry," the macaw said as he scooted along his perch. "Mervin hungry."

"He's always hungry." Bear retrieved a jar that was out of Rae's reach from her petite height. He took out a couple of parrot treats. "You can feed him these and he'll be happy."

Rae took the treats from him and Bear opened up the cage door. "If you hold out your arm, he'll sit on your shoulder."

She looked at Bear with a wary gaze. "I've never done that. Do his claws hurt?"

He shook his head. "He's gentle."

She held her arm out in the cage. Mervin scooted onto her arm and up to her shoulder. She fed Mervin a treat.

"Pretty lady feed Mervin." He bobbed his head. "Thank you, pretty lady."

Rae laughed. "He's a flirt."

Bear grinned. "He likes you."

"That's because I gave him cashews and now treats." She fed Mervin the second treat and the bird thanked her again.

"Would you like a glass of iced tea?" he asked.

"I would love one." Rae let Mervin return to his cage and Bear fastened it.

BEAR POURED each of them a tall glass. He took his tea with lemon, no sugar. Rae preferred lemon with sugar in hers.

He watched her drink from her glass, admiring her graceful neck as she swallowed her tea. Everything about her was beautiful.

She lowered her glass and caught him staring at her. He set his own glass on the island, trying to keep the moment from being awkward.

"I'll fire up the grill." Bear inclined his head to the back patio that she could see through the arcadia door.

"I'll go with you."

His backyard had a nice-sized lawn and trees as well as flowers, including hibiscus and lantana. She watched as he prepared a mesquite wood fire in the grill, and they returned to the house.

"I need to feed Arthur as well as the cats." He reached into the fridge and got out a can of a prescription rice and chicken formula dog food that would be gentle on his stomach. He put a portion in a bowl and put the lid on the can and returned it to the fridge.

"I'd like to feed him." She took the bowl once he'd handed it to her, knelt, and opened the kennel. The dog gave a much happier doggy smile, telling them he was feeling better. He gobbled up his food in no time flat. Bear gave him clean, fresh water.

He got liver paté out of the cabinet and opened the can. As he'd expected, his two cats came running into the kitchen.

Rae's eyes widened. She remained kneeling in front of Arthur's kennel, clearly not wanting to startle the cats. "They're beautiful. And huge. How do you grow them that big?"

He spooned half the can into Maggie's cat bowl and the other half into Katie's. "They're of the ragdoll breed. Very sweet and loving, and very big."

She nodded. "I'll say."

Bear put the bowls down for the mewling cats. "Meet Maggie." He pointed to the black cat with white patches. "And Katie." He gestured to the white with black cat.

"Can I pet them?" she asked.

"Sure." He gave a nod. "They're sweet. Just a little shy at first, but now that they're out they'll be somewhere around the rest of the evening."

Rae moved between the cats. They allowed her to stroke their soft fur without looking away from their food.

"What can I do to help?" she asked as she stood, just as he reached into the fridge for fresh vegetables.

"You can slice the peppers and I'll take care of the onion." He gave her a cutting board and knife with a red bell pepper and a yellow one.

He liked how comfortable it felt with Rae in his kitchen, as natural as if they'd done this a hundred times.

"What were you like in school?" Rae cut off the top of the red bell pepper and removed the seeds. "Were you always the good kid in class?"

Bear laughed. "With my brothers, there was no chance of *not* getting into trouble."

"Yeah?" She cocked her head. "What kind of trouble did you get into?"

"What *didn't* we do?" He grinned as he thought about it. "One time, Brady and I got a hold of a roll of toilet paper and wrote on it, 'Help! I'm trapped in a toilet paper factory!' We managed to get it into the teachers' restroom. One of my better ideas, if I do say so myself."

Rae grinned. "Somehow I can't see you as a prankster."

"You'd be surprised." He winked at her. "I instigated our pranking a few times myself. Once, we took all of the TP from the janitor's closet and hid it in an empty classroom. That was Brady's idea."

Smiling, she shook her head as she cut up the second pepper. "Okay, what else did you hooligans do?"

"We went into the lunchroom when the staff was gone and put faces on all of the eggs with a black marker—my idea." Bear grinned at the memory. "Another time we went back into the lunchroom and put sugar in the saltshakers and salt in the sugar jars, something Brady decided we should do. We got caught before we could leave."

"So, you have an ornery side." She met his gaze and smiled. "Who'd have thought?"

"Our parents," Bear said. "They could tell you stories and probably will."

Rae didn't respond and focused on the zucchini she was now cutting up.

The realization hit him that he'd just sounded like he assumed she would be meeting his mom and dad and he didn't know what else to say.

After a pause, he cleared his throat as he tried to recover. "Grandma and Grandpa tell plenty of stories about Dad that lets anyone know where we got it from."

"What about your sisters?" Rae finished slicing the squash. "Did they get into trouble?"

"Haylee and Leeann did." Bear put the sliced onion onto a large stoneware baking platter and added the peppers and zucchini that Rae had cut up. "Jill was what we called a goody-two-shoes. But really she was too busy doing well in school and reading library books to get into trouble like the rest of us."

"Why don't I set the table?" Rae said.

He told her where to find everything. She put plates, forks, and napkins on the placemats on the table in the kitchen nook.

Bear reached into the fridge and brought out two foil-wrapped packages of sliced buttered potatoes along with a package of steaks and set it all on the counter. "How do you like your steak?"

"Medium." She watched as he put the steaks onto a tray, along with grilling utensils.

"The stoneware is kind of heavy." He picked up the vegetable-laden stoneware platter and the foil packages of potatoes.

"I can get the tray." She grasped it and followed Bear outside.

The air smelled of burning mesquite wood and smoke rose into the air. He placed the stoneware baking platter beside the foil packets on a shelf in the grill then took the tray from Rae and set it on a sideboard.

He stirred the veggies on the stoneware as they grilled. "Did you and your sister get into any mischief while you were growing up?"

"Quite a few times after our parents died and we went to live with Grandmother." She watched him as she spoke. "Not so much pranks, but things like skipping class and writing notes supposedly from our grandmother. On some occasions we got caught and others we got away with it."

Bear set the grilling fork on the tray. "That's not so bad."

"Yeah, but the times Grandmother found out we got it worse than teenagers should." She leaned her hip against the sideboard and crossed her arms. "We continued to do it anyway. I guess that was our way of rebelling against her."

Bear thought about it. He hadn't done much rebelling, just got into mischief with his brothers.

They talked as Bear grilled their dinner. When it was finished, they carried the food back into the house. They filled their plates, grabbed their drinks, and sat at the table.

"I suppose I should have fixed a salad," he said as he took his seat. "It's something I should do more of."

"That's just rabbit food." Rae smiled as she picked up her fork and knife. "This is perfect."

He chuckled and cut into his steak.

"Wonderful." Rae had an expression of pleasure on her face as she chewed a bite of her steak. She tried the veggies and the foil-wrapped potatoes and pronounced everything perfect.

"Glad you like it." He smiled and continued to eat his rare steak and veggies.

Bear shared more stories about his youth, which Rae seemed to genuinely enjoy. She held back in regard to her own past, but he understood it considering what she'd told him about her grandmother, as well as her parents' deaths.

"Are you planning on staying with your cousin for a while?" he asked as he worked on his second helping of grilled vegetables.

Rae shrugged. "I'm not sure."

"What made you decide to leave the real estate business?"

She stilled, as if his question upset her, but recovered. "I needed a change in my life."

"Are you planning to continue to bartend, or do you have your eyes set on something else?"

"I haven't decided." She stared at her plate as she toyed with her potatoes. "You never know what can happen in life to change your perfectly laid plans."

He tried to hide a frown of concern and drank the rest of his third iced tea. His question had somehow upset her. Best change the subject.

"We have a Fourth of July festival coming up not too long from now." He used his napkin and set it down. "Are you planning on going?"

"I saw signs for it at the library." She met his gaze. "By the sound of it, planning starts early, and it looks like it's kind of a big deal around here."

"It is." He nodded. "Everyone gets into the celebration."

She cocked her head to the side. "What goes on during the festival?"

"Main street is closed off and the street has vendors selling pulled-pork sandwiches, hamburgers, candy apples, ice cream, and homemade fudge." He could almost taste it now. "We have a parade, of course. Then there's a pie eating contest and a hotdog eating contest. We have some games, too, like knocking down milk bottles with baseballs and go-cart races." He grinned. "And they always set up a dunk tank. People line up to try and dunk the mayor. At night there's fantastic fireworks."

"That all sounds like fun." She smiled. "I'll plan on going."

"Would you like to go with me?" He studied her as he hoped

he wasn't pushing her. "I can show you all the best parts of the festival."

She played with the end of her ponytail, wrapping it around her finger. "I think that sounds like a lot of fun, Bear. Sure, I'd love to."

"Great." He felt so dang good, like he could take on anything. He pushed away his empty plate. She'd finished her meal while he'd had seconds. "Ready for red velvet?"

"That will be a perfect way to top off a wonderful meal." She smiled. "I'll get the plates and forks, since I know where they are."

"I have vanilla ice cream to go with it, so how about spoons and bowls?" he said.

"Awesome," she said.

Rae stood and Bear got to his feet. He carried the dirty plates and forks to the sink and set them beside it. Rae retrieved the bowls and spoons and carried them to the table.

He got out the ice cream and handed it to Rae before he reached into a drawer for a cake server and an ice cream scoop. He took the cake out of the pink box and carried it all to the table. Bear sliced the cake while Rae served the ice cream.

Maggie and Katie showed up and sat at the foot of the table.

Bear pointed to them. "They love anything made from milk. I'm afraid I spoil them a little. Sometimes I give them each a teaspoonful." He spoke directly to them. "This is not one of those times. Go on, girls."

They both mewed, but Bear returned his attention to Rae and the cats retreated under the table. One of them wound around his legs and he could feel the cat's purr. Probably Maggie—she had the biggest purr of the two of them.

"Oh, my God." Rae sighed with pleasure after her first bite of the rich, red cake. "Best red velvet cake, ever, after my mom's. A *real* red velvet cake like how I remember Mom's Southern recipe. Not a chocolate cake with red food coloring like you get at the store."

He couldn't help but grin at her enjoyment. When she was who he thought was the true, genuine, happy Rae she had a sweet, openness about her. When she was guarded, he wasn't sure he'd really be able to get to know the real Rae.

Down beneath it all, he was certain he could see that person dying to stay out.

He wanted to talk with her about the things she was holding inside. He wanted to listen as she shared whatever it was that bothered her. But he'd only known her for a couple of days, and he knew it was far too soon for her to feel comfortable opening up to him.

Rae set her spoon in her bowl after eating every bit of her cake and ice cream. She met Bear's gaze. "I'll help you clean up."

He could have told her he'd take care of it, but she'd be leaving soon enough, and he wanted to keep her here as long as she was willing to stay. And, if she was anything like the members of his family, she liked to pitch in after enjoying a good meal.

He wiped down the island and counters with a wet cloth. Then, he handed her a drying towel as he filled the sink with soapy water. "I'll wash. You dry and set everything on the island, and I'll put it away."

She gave a nod. "Deal."

He rinsed remnants of food off the plates and bowls before putting them in the soapy water. He washed a plate and rinsed off the soap. "Do you miss snow? I imagine you got some when you lived in Albuquerque."

"I do miss it, some." She dried the plate he'd washed and rinsed. "If I remember correctly, we got about ten inches a year, although at most it would snow maybe three inches in a month." Her expression told him she was enjoying a memory. "Carrie and I would build snow forts and have snowball fights when we had a good snow."

"Did you make snow angels?" He handed her another washed and rinsed plate. "Go sled riding?"

She dried the dish. "It really depended on how good a snow we got since it's high desert there." With a smile, she went on. "Our mom liked to make snow angels with us, and our dad would take us higher in elevation to do a little sled riding." She sighed. "I miss those times."

"I bet you do." He cleaned a glass and rinsed it. "Our parents took us up to higher elevations and let us play in the snow sometimes. I think they liked to wear us out as much as possible."

Rae laughed. "I don't doubt it with five boys and three girls." She shook her head. "I can't imagine having a family that big."

"Don't knock it 'til you try it." He winked and she smiled.

He put the grilling tools into the soapy water and started cleaning them. "What did you like about living in Coyote Lake City?"

"It has its good points." She grasped the clean grilling fork he handed her. "Parts of it, like a lot of cities, are really nice while others not so much. The weather can be great from late fall to early spring, but so hot other parts of the year."

"What about the people?" he asked.

She shrugged. "Generally laid back compared to bigger cities. Although, for the last couple of years I sold pricier real estate and I would come across some of the most uptight people I'd ever met. I didn't feel that way when I sold less expensive properties."

"Most folks around here are laid back." He thought about Mrs. Clawson. "But there are some who are wound a little tighter than others."

When they'd finished washing and drying the dishes and had put them away, Bear said, "Would you like a wine cooler or a beer? I don't have any bottles of wine right now."

"I—" She hesitated several seconds, clearly debating. Finally, she said, "I'd like to, but it's getting late. I need to get back to Marlee's."

Disappointed, he glanced at the time on the microwave before returning his gaze to hers. "I didn't realize it's almost nine."

"My witching hour tonight." She smiled.

Bear retrieved her purse from the coatrack and walked her outside to her car. The night had cooled, the breeze sliding over his skin and causing loose strands of Rae's hair to get in her face. He wanted to brush them away but didn't. He'd probably already pushed things plenty far today.

Rae stood by her car door, and he found it hard to believe they'd just done this last night, only it was at Mickey's. Here they were, this time at his home.

She tipped her head and met his gaze. "I had a wonderful time today. I enjoyed our coffee, then coming out here and meeting all of your critters. It was a wonderful dinner, too."

"I'm glad you agreed to both." His voice came out huskier than he'd intended. "It's been a real good day."

She smiled. "It has."

Moonlight highlighted her fair skin, making her look like a beautiful doll. Damn, he wanted to kiss her.

Before he could think twice about it, he lowered his head and brushed his lips over hers.

He raised his head, afraid this time he really had pushed things too far.

But she was staring at him with eyes that told him she'd wanted more than just that simple, light kiss.

He moved toward her again, slowly, and she didn't move. When his lips met hers, she gave a soft sigh into his mouth.

His gut tightened and he grasped her slender shoulders as he moved his mouth over hers. It was a long, sweet, slow kiss, like nothing he'd ever experienced before.

When he raised his head, he wondered if he'd ever be able to catch his breath. Before he could press his luck, he said, "Good night, Rae."

"Good night," she said softly. "Call me tomorrow."

He gave a nod. "I will."

She stepped back and he opened her car door. In moments

she was sitting in the closed car, her window down. "Good night, Bear," she said again before backing up and heading down the road.

Bear blew out his breath. That was one hell of a woman, and somehow, he wanted to make this special woman his.

CHAPTER 7

Rae's gut felt lined with lead as she made the drive to Coyote Lake City to meet with her lawyer. Her mind churned over her upcoming appointment, which kept her mind occupied, and not in a good way.

Thoughts of her day with Bear made her smile, especially the memory of his kiss.

But then she deflated.

She hadn't answered her phone on Sunday. She kept it shut off completely, not wanting to see a call coming from him because she knew she'd answer it.

That she hadn't wanted to talk with him made no sense after the terrific day she'd spent with him on Saturday. Or maybe it did. Maybe she just needed to figure herself out before she could make a big mistake she'd regret—like falling for a cowboy when she had no intention of sticking around King Creek.

This morning she'd listened to a message he'd left, telling her he'd had a great day and that he'd like to see her again this week. Considering what she had to do today, she was not in a place mentally where she could call him back. Not yet.

She forced her thoughts away from him only to focus back on the trial and what she'd done. What she'd had to do.

By the time she sat in front of her attorney, Luther Deming, she thought she was going to be sick all over his luxurious carpet.

The slender but fit man seated himself behind his big glass-topped desk. He had a kind, paternal air when he spoke with her on a personal level. "How are you doing, Rae?"

She knew he was probably just asking to set her at ease, but with him she didn't feel that way. It was like he really cared how things were with her.

Rae mustered up a smile. "As well as can be expected, I guess."

He held a pen between the fingers of both hands. "Are you enjoying King Creek?"

She shrugged. "It's a nice little town. It's good to be away from here, where the locals don't know anything about me."

Luther gestured to her. "The new hairstyle and color do give you a different look."

She touched her hair. "I was thinking about cutting it shorter." She shifted in her chair. "Sorry, I know you've got more to be concerned about than how I look."

He studied her. "We do need to get you ready for trial." He looked at a yellow notepad on his desk before meeting her gaze again. "Prosecution is going to attempt to prove you encouraged Mr. Johnston to go to the houseboat when you left the bar. The prosecutor believes she can prove this."

A cold chill crept over Rae's skin. "I never—I did *not* ask that man to join me there." Her voice came out harsher than she'd intended.

"I believe you." Luther kept his gaze steady. "However, you need to be aware of the angle she's taking."

"He followed me without my knowledge." Tears stung the back of Rae's eyes, but she managed to hold them back. Things kept getting worse and worse. "How can the prosecutor prove otherwise?"

Luther set the pen down. "She has a witness."

Rae's eyes widened and her skin grew colder. "How? It never happened."

"One of Mr. Johnston's acquaintances is going to testify that he overheard you inviting Mr. Johnston to the houseboat."

"That's not possible." Rae shook her head violently. "I told Larry Johnston to get out of my face and I left the bar."

"I will destroy the witness on cross-examination, Rae." Luther's voice came out matter of fact. "We'll be prepared."

When Rae left her attorney's office, she felt even worse than when she'd arrived. How could anyone say she'd invited the bastard to go with her? She would never have done that in a million years. Larry was nothing but a sleazy S.O.B., who had tried to rape her and threatened to kill her when he followed her. She'd shot him because she'd been terrified for her life.

Had she done the right thing?

Hot tears flowed down her cheeks. She had thought she could injure him to stop him, but he'd tackled her to take away the gun. Her finger had been on the trigger when he'd knocked her on her back, and the gun had gone off in his gut.

Rae had called 911, but the man had bled out before the paramedics had arrived.

She had never set foot on the houseboat again.

Life had become nightmarish once the story broke. The media had gone all out, portraying her in an unkind light. Social media had blown up, saying to the world that she had asked for it. Larry Johnston's friends and family posted everywhere that she'd dressed like a tramp, she had been all over him, and on and on. If she had been a man, she would have been praised for protecting her home and for saving her own life. Instead, she was shamed and bullied and threatened. Signs with things like, "Murdering bitch lives here" had been driven into her front yard on several occasions.

Unlike her, Larry had grown up in Coyote Lake City, so he

had a lot of friends and family there. The hatred toward her had been unbelievable.

When she'd been arrested and charged, things got even worse. She'd felt humiliated and had nearly lost all hope. She'd been fortunate she'd been able to make bail, but that was small consolation.

Most of her clients had cancelled their contracts with her or asked to work with different agents. Few had wanted to continue working with a woman who had murdered a man in her home.

When it seemed like her life had fallen completely apart, she'd fled to King Creek at her cousin's urging and her sister's support.

And here she was, heading back to the small town to hide out a little bit longer, until the trial was over.

Rae prayed she wouldn't be behind bars when it was over.

Friday afternoon, Bear washed his hands after a difficult surgery as he mulled over the events from Saturday with Rae and the fact that she hadn't returned his call. He'd left a message Sunday when his call went straight to voicemail. He'd tried again Tuesday, but once again had to leave a message.

She'd probably been busy, but he didn't want to press her if she wasn't interested. Had he been reading her right Saturday? They'd had a great coffee date, and she'd agreed to come out to the ranch to meet his animals. He'd thought the day had only gotten better, and she appeared to be of the same mind.

Women. He never could figure them out.

Bear dried his hands and prepared to head home. His cell phone rang, and he fished it out of his lab coat. He glanced at his screen to see Colt calling.

He brought the phone to his ear. "Don't tell me you're calling to drag me to Mickey's." Truth was, if Bear had his way, he'd be hauling Colt there himself.

"Meet me there at eight. I'm hungry for one of Mickey's cheeseburgers."

Bear figured he'd turn the tables on Colt. "Don't be late."

Colt laughed. "Anxious to see that cute little redhead?"

Bear smiled. "Maybe."

If Rae didn't want to date him, he'd find out tonight. He might not have a way with women like Colt did, but he preferred to know where he stood with a woman. It just wasn't who he was, sitting around wondering. If she didn't want anything to do with him, better to know now.

"I'll see you there," Colt said. "You can tell me how Saturday went."

"Will do." Bear signed off and shrugged out of his lab coat. Colt was right—he was looking forward to seeing Rae and he hoped she'd be glad to see him.

BEAR WALKED through the entrance to Mickey's and he spotted Rae behind the bar at once. She served shots to a pair of regulars Bear knew well, but he only had eyes for Rae. She smiled at something one of the men said, gave a nod and turned away.

She glanced in his direction and she came to an abrupt stop in her turn. Her face seemed to light up when she saw him, giving him a warm feeling in his gut.

In the next moment, her expression shifted to one of concern and she turned away, like she was afraid of something.

Bear tried not to frown. What was that all about?

He recognized his brother's build and took the barstool next to him.

Colt turned his head. "Hey, bro. 'Bout time you showed up."

Bear didn't have to look at the neon Budweiser clock over the bar to know he wasn't late. "Save some onion rings for me?"

Colt pushed the half-eaten basket in front of Bear. "Got here early, so I figured I'd get started on something while I waited for your sorry ass."

Bear picked up an onion ring and dipped it in the ramekin of ranch dressing that Colt gave him. "Anything catch your attention while you've been waiting?"

Colt nodded in the direction of the pool table. "Cute little blonde over there been looking my way. Might go introduce myself." He glanced at Bear. "After I get started on that burger I've been waiting to order 'til you got here."

"Then let's get it ordered." Bear looked up and saw Rae nearing them. Warmth traveled straight to his belly again when she smiled.

"Hi, Bear." She turned her attention to Colt. "I see you've worked your way through most of those onion rings. Ready to order your burger?"

Colt gave a nod. "Make it a ranch burger, rare and loaded."

"You've got it." Rae turned her attention back to Bear and she smiled. "Hungry?"

His mind went places it had no business going when she asked him that. It wasn't food he was hungry for when he looked at her.

He cleared his throat. "I'll have the same thing as Colt."

"Beer?" she asked. "Same as last time? Domestic dark on tap?"

He raised his brows. "You remember?"

A smile touched her lips. "Of course."

"Make it two," Colt said, and Bear nodded.

"She definitely likes you." Colt looked at Bear after Rae left to take care of their food and drink orders. "I take it you had a good coffee date."

Bear moved his gaze from Colt to Rae's cute backside. "Good enough that she came out to the ranch to visit the animals and have dinner."

Colt slugged his shoulder. "Way to go, little brother."

Bear rubbed his arm as he glanced at Colt. "I called her and left messages, but she never called back."

Colt shrugged. "A guy never really knows what's going on in a woman's head. She might be playing hard to get or she might be just plain busy. Who the hell knows?"

Bear smiled at the easy way his brother spoke about it. "Maybe one of these days I'll get it right."

"Nope." Colt shook his head. "Just when you think you have figured out a woman, you learn you were all wrong. Just take it a day at a time—best you can do."

Bear glanced in Rae's direction again. "I think I have it bad for this one, Colt."

"You *know* you have it bad for her," Colt said as Bear continued to watch Rae. "No two ways about it."

Bear smiled at Rae as she carried two glasses of foam-topped beers and set the glasses down in front of them. Bear picked his up. "Thanks, Rae."

"You're welcome." She braced her palms on the bar top. "Ranch burgers will be up in about thirty. Busy night."

"I can see that." Bear glanced around before meeting Rae's gaze again. "It's only gonna get busier."

"Yeah, I have that feeling." Rae hesitated. "Sorry I didn't get a chance to call you back. It's been a kind of crazy week."

"No problem." Bear smiled. "Had a great day when you were out at the ranch. I think Mervin misses you. Keeps saying 'Where's pretty lady?' every time I walk into the kitchen."

Rae laughed. "I never expected you to be full of it."

"It's the gospel truth." Bear flashed her a grin. "You don't know Mervin very well, not yet."

Something flickered in her eyes, but her smile didn't fade.

"He's a sweet bird," she said.

"He sure thinks so," Bear said.

"I'd better get back to work." She nodded in the direction of the opposite end of the bar. "Hear my name being called."

Bear nodded and she turned away. He couldn't take his eyes off her backside. He liked the way she walked. Truth was, he liked everything about her—everything he knew about her, anyway. He had a feeling he'd like everything about her once he got to know her better.

Colt waved his hand in front of Bear's face. "Earth to Bear, come in Bear."

"You've got my attention." Bear picked up his draft. "Sorry. Can't keep my eyes off her."

"Can't say I blame you." Colt picked up his own beer. "Sounds like you had a nice time together Saturday."

"Yep."

"Is that crazy bird of yours really asking about 'pretty lady?'" Colt asked with amusement on his features.

Bear grinned but nodded. "Honest truth. Mervin really does like Rae."

He looked back at Rae and his grin melted to a frown. Cheeks flushed, lips tight, Rae stood in front of Bill and looked like she had a tough time not throwing his beer into his face. Bear didn't know what Bill was saying, but he sure didn't like how he was clearly making Rae feel.

Well, he was going to do something about it.

Bear climbed off his stool. "Be right back."

Colt nodded, his beer in his hand. "Go take care of her," he said, clearly understanding what Bear was doing.

He reached Bill who was saying to Rae "You know you want to. I'll be happy to pick up your cute little ass when you get off work."

Rae looked like she was about to explode and having a hard time holding it back.

Bear settled his hand on Bill's shoulder, trying not to give into his urge to clench down hard. "Bill, you need to treat this lady with respect."

Bill cut his gaze to Bear. "Mind your own business, McLeod." He pushed at Bear's hand, but he only increased his grip.

"Treat her like the lady she is," Bear said calmly.

Rae said nothing, just seemed to be frozen.

Bill climbed off his stool and glared at Bear. They stood toe-to-toe, both men topping six-two. Bill had twenty pounds on Bear, but Bear was a good ten years younger. He wasn't a fighting man, but he had a protective streak a mile wide.

"I'm gonna knock your fucking head off, McLeod. Get out of my way."

"Let's go outside and discuss this," Bear said. "Let the lady get back to work."

"It's okay, Bear." Rae sounded nervous. "I can deal with him."

Bear didn't look away from Bill. "Come on out. We'll have ourselves a little talk."

Bill looked like he was going to shove Bear, but Bear turned his back and walked to the bar's entrance. He knew Bill was an ass, but he also knew the man wouldn't hit him from behind.

"Bear, stop." Rae's anxiety grew in her tone.

He walked out the front door, off the porch, and out into the parking lot. He kept his arms loose at his sides.

Bill glowered in front of him. "I'm going to knock your goddamned head off. I don't care if you are a McLeod or the damned vet."

Bear eyed Bill steadily. "I didn't ask you out here to fight. I'm asking you nicely to leave Rae alone. She deserves to be treated like a lady, and from what I've seen today and last Friday, that's not what you're doing."

"You don't tell me how to treat no one." Bill clenched his fists and moved closer to Bear so that their chests almost touched. "I've had it up to here with your high and mighty ass acting like you're better than everyone else."

Behind Bill, Rae came out of the bar. "Stop. Bear."

"One more chance," Bear said quietly. "Leave her alone."

Bill swung his big fist.

Bear stepped aside in a quick and easy motion. Bill stumbled forward and landed face down in the gravel. He gave a roar of rage and scrambled to his feet.

"Stop, please," Rae shouted.

Bill charged Bear, who sidestepped him at the last moment. The man almost fell again. He spun around, his face purple with anger.

Colt stepped between the two. "Bill, give it up while you still can. No harm, no foul."

Bill's face twisted. "I'm gonna kick his ass. I don't care if he's your brother."

Colt held up his arm. "You don't know what you're getting yourself into. Bear hasn't even touched you. He's a martial artist and he can dance around you all day long."

With a surprised expression, Bill looked from Bear to Colt. "This goody-two-shoes doctor knows judo or some shit like that?"

Colt smiled. "Let me tell you, Bear is full of surprises."

Bill wiped his hands on the front of his jeans. "Well, hell." He looked like he had a whole new respect for Bear. "Know you're a good man, McLeod. Didn't know you could be a dangerous one."

Bear grinned. He knew Bill wasn't really worried about him and his martial art expertise. He was using it as an excuse to stop a fight he shouldn't have started.

He held his hand out to Bill, who took it. "Come on in. I'll buy you a beer."

Bill put his arm around Bear's shoulders. "You really know judo?"

Rae just stared at Bear as they neared her, eyes wide and her lips parted.

"Sorry, ma'am." Bill stopped in front of Rae looking

completely repentant. "I shouldn't let my mouth run off like it does sometimes."

Rae tore her gaze from Bear and looked at Bill. "Just don't do it again."

He bowed his head. "I won't. Promise."

"Sorry." Bear gave her an apologetic look. "Hope I didn't upset you. Just had to get him to cool off."

"Well, okay." She looked like she was totally flummoxed. "I need to get back to work." She turned and headed back inside.

Bear and Bill entered the bar followed by Colt and a couple of cowboys Bear knew who'd been watching in the parking lot. Bear sat and Bill took the stool next to him, while Colt returned to the other.

Rae brought over a beer and set it in front of Bill. "It's going on your tab," she said to Bear before turning away.

"Thanks, Doc," Bill said.

Bear glanced at Colt who was silently laughing. "You've got a way with women." Colt jerked his thumb in Bill's direction. "And asses."

"I heard that." Bill raised his beer. "To pretty ladies and vets who know judo shit."

"Taekwondo." Bear raised his own glass.

"Whatever." Bill took a big pull on his beer. "How'd you learn it? No judo place 'round here, unless you went up Phoenix way."

Bear didn't correct him again. "Learned it at a place in Tucson while I put myself through school at the U of A vet med college. I go to a Dojang in Chandler now."

Bill studied Bear. "You a Wildcat?"

"Yep." Bear took a swallow of his draft.

"Knew I liked you," Bill said. "Ain't no Sun Devil."

Rae brought their burgers and more beers.

Bear said, "When do you go on break, Rae?"

She looked at the clock over the bar. "Ten minutes."

"Mind if I join you?"

"Sure." She looked like she'd relaxed some since they'd come back inside. "Meet me out back in ten."

"I'll be there," Bear said.

Rae smiled before turning away.

CHAPTER 8

The clock above the bar seemed to drag. Rae wanted time to pass faster while at the same time she didn't.

At ten after, Rae told Patty she was on break.

The woman had a sour expression, like she was sucking on a lemon. "Don't be late getting back."

Rae held back a frown of her own. "No problem, Patty."

Bear wasn't sitting next to Colt, so he was probably outside. Despite all her reservations, she found herself smiling as she headed through the kitchen and out through the back door.

Bear stood beneath the light post's yellow glow. His western hat cast a shadow across his strong features, giving him a kind of tougher demeanor than the cowboy she'd been getting to know.

He pushed up the brim of his hat with one finger and moved toward her. The corners of his mouth turned up into a smile. "Thanks for meeting me on your break."

"Thank you for not fighting with Bill and getting him to stop bothering me." She pushed strands of hair out of her face that had been bothering her all night. "I know now he's harmless, but I've had some…bad experiences and he really got to me."

That she had "bad experiences" was truly an understatement.

Bear shrugged. "If I'd thought it would turn into a brawl, I wouldn't have taken it outside. But I know Bill, and sometimes he needs a little shove in the right direction to break his pattern."

"You're good with people," she said. "At dealing with and analyzing them."

"You haven't been around me enough to know that," he said with a smile. He moved closer to her, where she stood in the shadows.

"I'm a good judge of character." It was her turn to shrug. "Usually I have no problem dealing with different personalities, but guys who treat me like Bill did, not so much."

One had ended up dead. She really needed to get off this topic.

"Saturday was fun." She pulled her ponytail holder off so she could capture the loose strands and gather all her hair back. "Thank you again for inviting me."

The memory of his kiss came flooding back as he held her gaze and she wanted him to kiss her again. She took a step back so she wouldn't throw herself at him, begging for another kiss like the one they'd shared.

"It was my pleasure." His voice was low, husky. "The crew enjoyed meeting you."

"How's Arthur?" She heard a nervous edge in her voice. "Is he better?"

Bear nodded. "Up and getting around best he can. He's a good boy."

"Have you found his family?" she asked.

Bear shook his head. "Arthur is housebroken, so I'm thinking he has, or at least had, a home. I've been asking around and posted a couple of flyers, but I haven't heard from anyone yet."

"What will you do with him if you can't find his family?"

"I might take him in myself." Bear shoved his hands in his front pockets. "So far things have been okay with Katie and Maggie, but they've mostly stayed hidden when Arthur is out of his kennel. I need to make sure he's a good fit with all the animals and the ranch. If he's not, I'll make sure to find him a good home."

She cocked her head to the side. "What would make him a good or bad fit for the ranch?"

"If he chases my cattle or horses, and he's not easily trained to behave, that's an out for a ranch," Bear said. "If he barks at the animals or tries to attack any of them, he's not a good fit. I can only do so much training with my schedule, and I need to know that when I'm not home, he gets along with all of the animals." He hooked his thumbs in his front pockets. "Whatever the case, I'll make sure he ends up with a good home."

"That all makes sense." Rae wanted to close the distance between them, so that her breasts would brush his chest and he'd take her face in his hands. And kiss her. She swallowed back the urge. "You have a lot of pets to consider when you bring another in."

He fixed his gaze on her mouth, like he was thinking of kissing her.

The other night had been so sweet. She wanted it so badly, she could almost feel his lips on hers.

Despite herself, she moved closer to him. He was so much taller than her, she had to tip her head back.

A hungry expression crossed his sexy features. Unable to stop herself, she placed her hands on his chest, and she could feel his body heat through her touch.

He slid his fingers to the back of her head, cupping it in his big palm. He rested his other hand on her hip and drew her against him.

Rae caught her breath as he lowered his mouth to hers. The moment their lips touched, she gasped into his mouth.

He gave a low groan and he slid his tongue between her lips. She kissed him back, needing him in a way she'd never needed anything or anyone in her life. His kiss and his arms wrapped around her were both exciting and healing. Like this man could take her places she'd never been to before and keep her safe while doing it.

The door slammed open behind them and Rae startled and jumped back. Bear slid one arm around her shoulders, as if protecting her as she turned to see Patty standing on the doorstep, glaring.

"Can I help you?" Rae managed to keep her voice steady.

Patty put her hands on her hips. "Couldn't wait to start screwing around with the local cowboys?"

Heat rushed to Rae's cheeks and she clenched her fists into hands.

Bear stepped from the shadows, into the light. "Hi, Patty. How's Biff?"

Patty's jaw dropped and she looked like she'd just lost her best friend. "Hi, Doc." She appeared to be gathering herself. "My dog's fine."

Bear kept his arm around Rae's shoulders. "Good to hear."

Patty cleared her throat and raised her chin as she turned her gaze on Rae. "You're late. We need you back inside."

Rae frowned. "It's been fifteen minutes?"

"Yes." Patty's reply was sharp. She looked back at Bear. "See you, Doc." The woman stepped back into the bar and closed the door behind her.

Rae let out her breath. "That was painful."

Bear chuckled. "Like her dog, Biff, Patty's bark is worse than her bite."

"If you say so." Rae sighed and smiled at Bear. "I've got to go."

He brushed his lips over hers. "I'll wait for you after the bar closes."

She blew out her breath. "Okay." She turned, glanced over her shoulder and smiled at Bear, then hurried back into the bar.

When Rae got back behind the bar, Patty glared at her. "In the future, don't be late from break if you want to keep your job."

Rae drew herself up to her full five-two and stared down the woman who was a good five inches taller. She kept her voice low so she wouldn't be overheard by the patrons. "Patty, last I heard I answer to Mickey. You have my apologies for making you late to your break, but don't threaten me again."

"Tramp." Patty ground the word out beneath her breath as she spun and left.

Rae found she'd been holding her breath as Patty exited the room. She blew it out and returned to tending bar.

She glanced in Bear's direction and couldn't help a smile when she saw the tall, sexy cowboy watching her. He returned her smile and she wanted to kiss him all over again.

The rest of the evening was so busy, she didn't have much more time to even look in Bear's direction. She did stop by to see if he, Colt, or Bill needed anything else. Bill had said he didn't, slid off his stool, and paid his tab before leaving.

Colt and Bear didn't order anything else. Bear just gave her his sexy little grin while Colt looked amused.

At closing time, Mickey got everyone to leave the bar. Rae Patty, and Jane took care of clean-up and then it was time to head on out.

Rae's heart beat a little faster as she went out to the parking lot. Bear was leaning up against her sportscar, hands in his front pockets, waiting for her.

When she reached him, he took her by the shoulders and lightly brushed his lips over hers. She shivered, loving the feel of his lips and the power of being in his presence.

He raised his head and smiled. "Ready to head home? Bet you're dead on your feet, as hard as you work."

She shrugged as she tried to keep from yawning. "I'll be glad to climb into my bed and sleep late. Friday nights do get busy and I've got to work Saturday, too."

He reached up and played with her ponytail that was lying

over her shoulder. "As much as I don't like to see you go, I won't keep you."

She smiled at the way he made her feel needed and wanted. "I don't mind waiting a little bit longer before I go home."

His eyes were shadowed by the brim of his hat. "What do you think about dinner out on Sunday?"

She cocked her head as she thought about it. She usually did all she could to avoid being in public. Who knew if someone would recognize her?

"Would it be okay if I come over to see your furry and feathered family instead? Maybe I can ride Angel." She put her hand on his chest, feeling his body heat through her touch. "I could bring out Chinese or Mexican."

"That will be perfect. He put his hand over hers. "But I pay for dinner."

She shook her head. "I know you cowboys have strong feelings about taking care of women, but let me do this, okay? Next time you can pay."

Her cheeks burned as she realized she'd just assumed there would be a next time.

Bear smiled, as if pleased to hear her assumption. "I'll take care of dessert."

"Good." She gave him a teasing grin. "Bet you can't beat that red velvet cake."

"I'll do my best." He flashed her a grin. "I sure did enjoy the leftovers."

Rae laughed. "I'll just bet you did."

"Did you find out if Marlee has a pair of boots you can borrow?" Bear asked.

"She does." Rae nodded. "We wear about the same size shoe, so they'll work."

"I'm glad you're coming to my place Sunday." He stroked her cheek lightly as he looked into her eyes. "It's nice having you there."

"I enjoyed my visit last weekend." She swallowed as his mouth neared hers. "I—"

He covered her mouth with his and she didn't get to finish what she was going to say. As a matter of fact, she couldn't even remember a word of whatever it was.

His kiss was so sweet and powerful, a combination that stirred wild feelings inside her. Dear God, she loved the way he kissed.

When he drew back, she tried to catch her breath. "Keep that up and I won't be able to sleep tonight." She didn't know why she'd said that, but the way it came out made her cheeks burn again. "I mean—"

He kissed her, and she sank into him. This man sent every rational thought out of her mind. He made her forget all the bad and all she felt around him was good.

He raised his head. "I'm gonna send you home now so you can get some good sleep."

She wanted to stay right where she was, in his arms. She smiled. "I'll be there Sunday, around noon. Make sure you have a good appetite."

"Looking forward to it." He kissed the top of her head before opening her car door for her. She climbed in and lowered her window. She started the car and blew him a kiss before she headed home, wondering what the hell she was doing.

Falling for a man she definitely shouldn't be falling for.

CHAPTER 9

"The food smells great." Bear set the takeout bags on the kitchen nook table, Rae following in his wake, her unfamiliar boots clunking on the tile floor.

"Try driving for twenty minutes smelling that." She placed two Styrofoam cups filled with Coke on the table. "My stomach was rumbling the whole way."

Rae greeted Arthur, who was in his kennel. Bear let him out and Rae crouched to give Arthur the hug she'd promised him. She was careful not to grip too tightly to make sure she didn't hurt him.

She smiled up at Bear. "Arthur looks like he's doing well."

"He is." Bear rubbed Arthur behind his ears. "He's well-trained, which makes me certain he has or at least had a family somewhere."

Rae gave Arthur another affectionate hug before getting to her feet. Arthur plopped down on the dog bed near the old-fashioned coat stand.

She went to Mervin and peered in at the macaw. "How are you, Mervin?"

Mervin scooted on his perch, closer to her. "Hi, pretty lady."

Rae laughed. "You're such a cute bird."

"Cute bird," Mervin said. "Cute bird."

Still smiling, Rae faced Bear as he got a couple of forks out of the silverware drawer and took them to the table. They seated themselves and Bear opened the containers, each one filled with an enchilada, a taco, and a tostada.

She took the container he offered her and cut into the enchilada. "Marlee raves about this restaurant."

"Ricardo's is one of those hole-in-the-wall places you can't beat." Bear crunched his taco and chewed before drinking his Coke.

Rae munched happily on her lunch, her heart feeling lighter than it had in a long time. Bear made her feel that way, her past seeming so remote that it couldn't touch her when she was with him.

He finished his taco. "Are you ready to ride Angel?"

Rae stuck her foot out to the side. "I've got Marlee's boots, so that part of the equation is there." She lowered her foot before picking up one of the paper napkins that had been in the takeout bag. "I loved being in the saddle last time, but I'm nervous about going outside of the corral."

"We don't have to," Bear said. "We'll stay in the corral or in the pasture and let you ride Angel until you feel confident. Then, we'll go from there."

Rae took a bite of her tostada. "I enjoyed my time with Angel last weekend, so I think I'll be okay. I just want to make sure I can handle her."

"She's a good horse, and you did well with her," Bear said. "You'll be just fine."

They finished their lunch and put the container with Rae's leftover taco in the fridge. After deciding to save dessert for later —whatever it was Bear had gotten—they put Arthur in the kennel and headed out to a grassy pasture, where Angel and Roxie were grazing.

The day was hot again, but clouds gathered over the Superstition Mountains. Being monsoon season, they could end up getting a good rain, even if the weather report claimed it would be hot and sunny. The weather reports were less accurate during monsoon season in Arizona.

When they reached the pasture fence, Rae climbed onto the bottom rung and put her arms on the top rail to watch the beautiful and majestic creatures. Bear whistled and both horses looked up then trotted toward Bear and Rae.

Roxie reached Bear and bumped her nose into his hat, knocking it back, but not off. Bear adjusted it before stroking her forehead. Angel snuffled Rae's hair, the mare's warm breath tickling her scalp. She laughed and patted Angel's nose.

Bear grasped two nylon lead ropes hanging from a hook near the gate. "Let's get these girls saddled up."

Rae couldn't help feeling a bit nervous about getting on the back of such a huge animal again. It had been exciting, but she still had her reservations.

He clipped a lead on Angel's halter and handed it to Rae. She led the palomino to the barn while Bear followed with Roxie.

Once in the barn, Bear observed while Rae saddled Angel. He answered her questions and made encouraging remarks as she did her best to follow the instructions he'd given her last weekend. When she finished, he looked over her handiwork, made a couple of adjustments, and told her she'd done a great job. Rae glowed under his praise, not sure why it made her feel as good as it did.

Bear saddled Roxie, then boosted Rae up into Angel's saddle. Her foot did feel more secure in a boot as she slipped it into the stirrup.

He handed her the reins and she gripped them 'til her knuckles ached as she tried to pull her nerves together.

Bear rested his hand on her thigh and smiled. "Ready to go out for a little ride while I'm on Roxie?"

Rae tried to ignore the tingling in her belly from the way he had his hand on her thigh, just like last time.

She focused on her current position. It was so high, sitting on Angel, and a long way to the ground. Last time Bear had been standing beside the horse the whole time she'd been in the saddle. It would be different with him sitting on Roxie.

She met his gaze. "If something happens, will you be able to help me while you're on Roxie?"

He gave a single nod. "I've been riding my whole life. You'd be amazed what you can do from the back of a horse."

"Okay." Rae took a deep breath. "I'm as ready as I think I can get."

"Remember the instructions I gave you on controlling Angel?" Bear asked.

"I think so." Rae stared at the reins she held so tightly. "I could use a refresher."

He went over everything again with her, to make sure she had it. "Angel will stay close to Roxie, another reason why I'm not concerned about her taking off on her own."

When they both felt confident about the basics of her learning to ride, Bear gripped the bridles of both horses and walked them outside the barn. He closed the barn doors, then mounted Roxie.

Rae's stomach flipped. "Are we going to the corral?"

"Let's try the pasture." He tipped his head in that direction. "Ready?"

She nodded.

He clicked his tongue and Roxie started forward. Angel fell into step beside Roxie as Rae made the correct movement with her reins.

She was amazed at the smoothness of Angel's gait, despite rocking in the saddle. When they reached the pasture, Bear dismounted, opened the gate and let them in before closing the gate behind them.

He mounted Roxie in an easy movement. "How're you doing?"

She smiled. "I think I could get the hang of this."

"That's my girl." He returned her smile. "Why don't you start first?"

Rae clicked her tongue like Bear had at the same time she signaled with the reins that she wanted Angel to go forward.

The horse started moving. A surprisingly triumphant sensation went through Rae at the fact she was controlling the animal, or at least felt like she was.

Bear clicked his tongue and kept his horse alongside hers. "You're looking good."

She stared ahead at the expanse of the grassy pasture. "Maybe I'll be able to go a little faster." She glanced at Bear. "In the future, I mean. I'm not feeling that confident yet, mind you."

"All in good time." He looked ahead. "Clouds are building over the Superstitions."

She looked in the same direction. "It's such a beautiful mountain range. Like the Almighty planted them in the middle of the desert for the spectacular view."

Bear chuckled. "That's a good way of describing it."

"I like it in this part of the state." Her gaze swept the scenery from one side to the other. "The Coyote Lake City area is beautiful, too."

"Why did you leave?" Bear asked in a low tone.

"I needed a change." She cast him a quick glance before looking away again. She knew she should tell him why, but she didn't want to taint the beautiful day and her time with Bear.

Another thought sobered her. Bear was such a sweet man. Was she tainting him with the darkness surrounding her? He didn't deserve to be caught up in what she was dealing with.

"Rae?" Bear's concerned voice drew her out of her dark thoughts. "Are you all right?"

She turned her attention to him and forced a smile. "I'm fine."

"If you need to talk, I'm a good listener," he said.

"I'm sure you are." She looked ahead. "But really, I'm okay." She met his gaze again. "Can we go faster?"

"Do you remember how to tell Angel you'd like to pick up speed?" he asked.

She nodded and he told her, "Go on, now."

Rae used the reins just like he'd shown her, and Angel started moving at a faster pace. The exhilaration Rae felt surprised her. A breeze from movement stirred the warm air and caused tendrils of hair to rise from around her face.

She grinned at the feeling of excitement that coursed through her. She glanced at Bear, who smiled at the enjoyment that had to be clear on her features. "This is awesome."

"I think you're ready to go for a ride outside the pasture," he said. "We can save it for next time. What do you think about a ride and a picnic?"

"Sounds like a lot of fun." She relaxed in the saddle. "What a difference in how I feel now than I did last weekend. It's like a switch inside me flipped from terrified to excited."

"You look more confident." He swept his gaze over her. "You're more comfortable on Angel's back and your posture is excellent."

She basked in the warmth of Bear's praise and observations. He was the expert and a man who wouldn't say anything he didn't actually feel. She could read people, and Bear was an easy man to understand.

The man she'd killed had been an easy read, which was why she hadn't wanted anything to do with him. She just hadn't counted on him following her home to get even with her for telling him to take a hike.

The pleasure she'd been feeling slipped away at the memory. A burst of anger flared through her that the man had made ruins of her life, even though he wasn't around anymore. She'd picked herself back up, but she faced uncertainty in her future, all thanks to him.

"What's wrong, Rae?" Bear's tone was firm this time as he asked the question. "You were as happy as anyone I've seen, and then ten seconds later, you're clearly upset."

Her throat worked as she looked away from him. "I'm sorry."

"About what?" Bear asked. "Talk to me."

"I don't want to ruin the day." The words that came out surprised her. She met his gaze. "I promise I'll tell you about it. Just not today. Okay?"

He gave a slow nod. "I don't want to pressure you, but I know you need someone to talk to, and you know I'm here for you."

A lightening of the pressure of telling him made her relax a little. "Thank you."

"Want to move a little faster?" he asked her. "As long as you stay focused on the horse, I think you're ready."

She smiled. "I'd love that." She used the reins to give Angel the signal to pick up her pace. Angel did, and for a moment, Rae wondered if she'd pushed herself too far too fast. But then she started to enjoy herself again. She shoved away all thoughts that weren't good ones.

The beautiful day was filled with sunshine, a sexy man, and a gorgeous horse. Life couldn't get any better, could it?

In between Rae practicing commands with Angel, they chatted and laughed as they rode, talking about family and also about the regular and more unusual people she'd met so far in the bar.

"There definitely are a lot of characters in this town," she said.

Bear nodded his agreement. "And you've only met a few."

She studied him for a moment. "I still think that was amazing, how you handled Bill. He was in again on Saturday night, and he was as nice and respectful as he'd been after his sort-of fight with you."

Bear shrugged. "I think you handle yourself well in that bar. Bill just needed a wake-up call when it came to you. I don't know that it'll make him any more respectful with other women, but at least he shouldn't bother you again like he was."

"You don't know how much I appreciate what you did," she said.

"It was no problem," he said.

Rae shifted in the saddle, leaned forward, and patted Angel's neck.

"We should probably call it a day," Bear said after riding for some time around the pasture. "You're going to be sore as it is since you're not used to riding yet."

"Okay." She guided Angel toward the gate. "I'm looking forward to the ride and picnic."

He glanced at her. "How's next weekend?"

"Sunday would be good." Rae brought Angel to a halt at the pasture gate. It was starting to feel more natural riding the beautiful mare.

He brought Roxie to a halt beside Angel. "Ten sound good to you? That'll give us a chance to ride some before we have lunch."

She nodded enthusiastically. "Perfect. I can make lunch."

He shook his head. "You brought lunch today. I'm handling lunch on Sunday."

Rae smiled. "Then it's my turn for dessert."

"Deal." He swung down in a graceful movement then opened the pasture gate.

Rae encouraged Angel to walk through the gate and brought her to a stop on the other side. She waited for Bear to bring Roxie through and close the gate behind him.

Bear mounted his horse again. "You've come a long way in learning how to ride," he said. "You should feel proud of yourself."

"I have a fantastic teacher," she said, while wondering if she deserved to feel this happy with a man who didn't deserve to be marred by the ugliness she faced.

Again, she threw off the feelings. Today was for fun. She'd worry about the bad when she was alone.

Rae enjoyed brushing down Angel after removing her saddle and blanket, and it seemed that Angel liked it, too. Rae talked with Angel, telling her what a good horse she was and that she was looking forward to their ride next time.

After she'd been talking to the horse for a while, she realized Bear wasn't talking to Roxie anymore. She glanced in his direction and found him watching her.

Sweet heat and more flowed through her as his lovely hazel eyes drank her in. "Are you finished with Roxie?" Her voice sounded throaty as she spoke.

"I am." He patted the mare's neck. "Looks like you're about done with Angel."

"Yes." Rae wrapped her arms around Angel's neck and rested her face against her. "She's a lovely animal."

Bear moved to Rae's side and she tipped her head back to look into the tall man's eyes.

He lowered his head and brushed his lips over hers. When he drew back, he said, "You did great today." The husky note in his voice sent a shiver through her.

"I feel like teacher's pet," she said, and he laughed.

They put up and fed the horses, and then she helped him take care of the ducks, chickens, and rabbits.

The cattle showed up while they were feeding the other animals. She hadn't had a chance to meet any of the cattle.

"They're Herefords," Bear explained as they stood outside the eastern pasture, as opposed to the southern pasture where she'd ridden Angel. "Herefords have red coats and white faces."

She leaned her hip against a fencepost. "Did you name all of them?"

He shook his head. "They're not pets so I don't give them names. I raise them for beef and to sell to the 4-H kids."

Rae slowly nodded. "I see."

He turned away from the pasture. "Let's head back to the house."

When they walked into Bear's kitchen, he let Arthur out of the kennel. Rae got down and sat cross-legged, leaning forward to hug and pet the dog.

"He's good-natured and friendly." Rae looked at Bear who had squatted beside her. "I wonder what happened to his family."

Bear shook his head. "No telling. I've put up signs in town and asked around, but no luck in finding any clues to who he belongs to. Like I said before, he's thin and he was scraggly when you found him, so it's likely he's been on his own for a while."

Rae stroked the dog's head. "He's looking so much better."

"He's resilient," Bear said. "It's hard to keep him settled down, but his injuries remind him."

"You're such a good boy, Arthur." She held his head in her hands as she looked into the beautiful brown eyes. "Now you just need to prove you can behave around livestock and small stock, and you might find yourself the perfect home."

"Ready for the dessert I promised you?" Bear asked.

She perked up. *"Yes."* She scooted to her knees, then got to her feet as Bear stood.

Arthur followed her to the table and curled up at her feet as Bear finally unveiled dessert. He set it on the table between them. "Homemade cherry pie."

"My favorite." Rae clasped her hands. "I'm in love."

Bear chuckled. "That was easy."

"Oops." Rae's face warmed. "I'm in love with the pie."

"Too late," he teased.

"Seriously," she said as she tried to recover. "You made this?"

"My sister-in-law, Kit, did." He flashed her a grin. "Sorry to disappoint you."

She rolled her eyes. "You couldn't disappoint me if you tried."

Bear took his seat. He cut slices of the delicious-looking pie and put each on a dessert plate.

Rae dug into hers. "This is amazing. I'm in love with Kit and I haven't even met her."

He smiled. "We're all in love with Kit's cooking and baking." He explained how she was a chef in L.A. before arriving in King Creek. "You'll have to ask her sometime how she ended up as a cook for a bunch of cowhands on Carter's ranch."

"Now that sounds like it could be an interesting story," Rae said.

She finished her pie and looked at Bear, who was watching her. "I know we just had dessert, but would you like to stay for dinner?" he asked.

Rae wanted to say, "Absolutely, yes," but instead she shook her head. "I have some things to take care of at Marlee's."

He looked disappointed but smiled at her.

She couldn't help but smile back at him, while wondering why she was letting things go so far.

Not true. She knew exactly why—she was coming to care for Bear more than she'd cared for any man in her life. "I'm looking forward to our ride and picnic next weekend."

"I am, too," he said. "I'll have our picnic lunch ready when you get here, and we'll have a nice ride up into the Superstitions."

She stood and picked up her plate and his. "I'd better get going."

He took the plates from her and carried them to the sink before he retrieved her purse off the coat stand and handed it to her. She slung it over her shoulder and looked down at the borrowed boots. "I have to admit I'm looking forward to getting these things off." She raised her eyes. "My feet are killing me."

"Soak them in Epsom salts." He walked with her to the door and opened it for her. "They'll feel lots better."

"I'll buy some on the way home at the pharmacy," she said. "Are they open on Sundays?"

"Yep." Bear nodded. "I'd send some home with you, but I ran out. I need to pick some up."

They walked side by side to her car. He opened the door for her, and she threw her purse inside.

Rae tipped her head to look into his eyes. "Thanks for the wonderful day, Bear."

He rested his palms on both her shoulders. "You did great today. I think you're going to enjoy the ride up into the Superstitions for our picnic."

She smiled. "I know I will."

He lowered his head and gave her one of the most amazing kisses of her life. Every kiss she shared with Bear was incredible, and she just couldn't help but feel like they got better and better every time."

When he drew back, she had a hard time breathing. "Bye," she said softly.

"Be careful driving home." He pressed his lips to her forehead before sliding his palms down her arms then letting them fall to his sides.

It seemed like she was always leaving. But the thing was, she kept coming back.

She climbed into her car, gave him a little wave, then drove back into town.

CHAPTER 10

Rae drove her car across the cattle guard and onto Black Bear Ranch.

Due to Bear's schedule and Rae's, they'd had to postpone their riding date for another couple of weeks, so today was finally the day.

The original date they were supposed to go, he'd had an emergency with a mare on a neighboring horse ranch. Rae had been disappointed, but during the prior days, Bear had come in each night she worked at the bar, and she'd gone out to a late lunch with him on Saturday, before she'd had to go into work.

Over the next two weeks, Bear and Rae had gone out to dinner at local restaurants, including Ricardo's. Bear came over to Marlee's for dinner one night, which had been fun. In between glasses of wine for Rae and Marlee, and a Guinness for Bear, her cousin and Bear told stories about their school years and had Rae in giggles throughout the night.

He continued to come into Mickey's on the nights she worked. She knew her face lit up every time he walked through the doors and his expression seemed to do the same.

She didn't get a lot of time to spend with him while she

worked, but they talked every break and he always waited for her after she got off work.

Every moment spent with Bear was uplifting. Rae had never felt like this in her entire life. He was such a good man and everything about him made her want to spend as much time with him as she could.

Sometimes what was bad in her world would intrude and she'd have to force it away with everything she had. The trial date was creeping closer, and with it a sense of dread.

But not today. She wouldn't allow anything to ruin her time with Bear. Now she would have a full day with him, just the two of them.

Bear walked out of the house as she parked and hugged her and gave her a big kiss when she got out. They headed inside the house and she greeted Mervin, Katie, and Maggie. Bear let Arthur out of the kennel and the dog wiggled with excitement despite his injuries.

Rae rubbed the dog behind his ears. "Look at you. You'll be running the range before we know it." She glanced at Bear before turning back to Arthur. "Providing you know how to behave yourself on a ranch."

Bear nodded. "He's a smart dog and I have a good feeling about him. I think he'll learn just fine."

"Can he go with us today?" she asked.

"I don't think that's a good idea just yet," Bear said. "His injuries haven't fully healed, and we'll be going out a ways from home. I also haven't seen if he'll behave around the horses, so that's always a concern."

"That makes sense," she said.

"Ready?" he asked.

She smiled. "Am I ever."

"My sister, Leann, left a hat here that you can use." Bear grabbed the straw western hat for her and pulled his own low on his brow.

"She won't mind?" Rae asked as she plopped Leann's hat on her head and adjusted it. The hat was about the right size, so it would work.

"Nah, she won't mind." Bear carried a saddlebag over his shoulder that he'd filled with their lunch and thermoses of water.

Rae saddled Angel and Bear checked over her work and pronounced she'd done a great job. She felt inordinately proud of herself.

The ride from the ranch, up into the Superstition Mountains, popularly referred to as "The Superstitions," was a pleasant one. Rae enjoyed talking with Bear about anything that came up, as long as it didn't come too close to what she had come to think of as her "secret." She'd have to tell Bear, but she wasn't ready, and she didn't want to ruin the time she shared with him.

The air was cooler when they reached the forest. During their ride, clouds had built up over the mountains, threatening to bring monsoon rains later in the day.

Bear found a nice area to tie the horses and lay out a blanket to have their picnic. He pulled the saddlebag he'd brought off Roxie and rested it on the blanket. Rae sat cross-legged on the blanket while Bear sat and began pulling out their lunch and the thermoses of water.

"Barbeque sandwiches." He laid plastic-wrapped thick slices of bread filled with beef, on the blanket. He pulled out containers of potato salad and cowboy beans and spooned out everything onto paper plates.

"You made all of this?" Rae set Leann's hat aside as she looked at the food with surprise. "It looks amazing."

"I'm a man of many talents," he said with a teasing grin as he set a plastic fork on her plate.

"So I'm learning." She smiled and unwrapped her sandwich.

"Has something to do with being a longtime bachelor and getting tired of boxed meals in college," he said. "Out of self-preservation, I had to start cooking. Fortunately, Mom taught us how. It was just a matter of putting that training to use, rather than taking the lazy way out, like I had in my younger days."

"I am much appreciative." Rae took a big bite of her sandwich and chewed. She swallowed and used the napkin Bear had laid on the blanket for her. "This is fantastic."

"Glad you like it." He bit into his own sandwich.

"I have a question for you." She held onto her sandwich. "How did you get the name 'Bear'?"

The corner of his mouth quirked. "I used to read to my youngest sister, Haylee, and she loved the story of *The Three Bears*. She started repeating "bear" around me because she wanted me to read it to her yet again. My brothers thought it was funny as hell, so they started in and it wasn't long before everyone was calling me Bear."

"That's cute," Rae said. "What's your real first name?"

"Bart William," he said. "But I've been called Bear so long I might not know who you're talking to if you call me Bart."

"You don't look like a Bart." She shook her head. "But that's probably why your sign at the clinic uses the initial 'B.'"

He nodded. "It's my legal name." He looked thoughtful. "Is Rae your full name, or is it short for something?"

"It's my name." She shifted on the blanket. "I was named after my great-grandma Rae Fox."

They continued to chat about family as they made their way through all of the delicious food.

After they ate, they stretched out on the blanket and stared up at the sky, which could be seen through gaps in the tree cover. They talked about his work and hers. They never seemed to have a time when they didn't know what to talk about. Rae found Bear incredibly easy to talk with. He was interested in so many things that she could talk for hours with him and never get tired of it.

She studied the clouds. "The sky is getting darker."

"Yep." Bear scooted to a sitting position. "We'd better get back."

Rae got up and scooped up the hat, put it back on her head, then helped Bear gather their things.

By time they were riding up to the ranch, the wind had picked up and thunder sounded in the distance.

A couple of raindrops landed on Rae's jeans and the back of her hand. "Looks like we made it just in time," she said as he got down and opened the pasture gate.

Raindrops fell faster as they reached the barn and lightning cracked the sky, causing Rae to shiver.

The shelter of the barn was a welcome relief. The drumming on the barn's roof grew louder while they put up the tack and brushed down the horses.

While they finished up with the horses, the rain stopped. Arizona monsoons could go as fast as they came.

Rae breathed deeply of the rain-scented air. "Smells wonderful."

He started toward the house. "Monsoon season is my favorite time of year. We just don't get enough rain around here."

"It feels like hours since we last ate." She fell into step beside him. "I worked up an appetite."

He flashed her a smile as they strode toward the backdoor of his home. "Can you stay for a light supper?"

"Sure." She met his gaze. "What do you have in mind?"

"I was thinking about BLTs." He shoved his hands in his front pockets. "I have a package of bacon from the butcher, fresh tomatoes and lettuce from my mom's greenhouse."

"What about mayo?" Rae spoke solemnly, as if it was the most important item of the day. "You can't have BLTs without a ton of mayo."

"I have at least a ton, if not more," he said with a teasing grin.

"Sold." She slid her hand into his, surprising herself, and from the look on his face, she'd surprised Bear as well.

He gripped her hand. "Just wait 'til you see dessert."

"I sure enjoyed the cherry pie." She smiled. "Can't wait to see what you'll pull off this time."

Rae excused herself to use the bathroom and freshen up. She liked Bear's home. It was comfortable and lived in, as well as attractive. Her practiced eye told her his home couldn't be more than ten years old. It had vaulted ceilings, wall-to-wall tile, tall windows, taupe-painted walls, and deep windowsills. The rooms that she'd seen had western-style furnishings and neutral tones. The place could use some houseplants, but other than that it didn't need much.

The guest bathroom had taupe and cornflower blue hand towels. She'd asked Bear if she could freshen up with a washcloth and towel, and he had told her where to find them. She smelled of horse and dust and felt grubby. After washing her face, hands, and forearms, she felt a lot better.

She started to leave the bathroom, but hesitated. She had been letting things progress with Bear farther than she had planned. Did she owe it to him to tell him that she'd killed a man, before she let things go farther?

Steve had dumped her, treating her as if she'd encouraged the attention from her attacker. But Bear would never do that, she was certain. More certain of that than anything else in her life.

Then why hadn't she told him? *It's too soon,* she told herself. But was it?

What about her intention to leave King Creek and Arizona and never come back?

The thoughts warred within her and it took her a few moments to gather herself before she opened the door and left the bathroom. She had no clear idea what to do. One way or another, she had to figure things out before it all drove her crazy.

The one thing she did owe to Bear was telling him about her plans to move to Albuquerque.

When she walked back into the kitchen, she smelled bacon

and heard it sizzling on the griddle. "I haven't had a BLT in ages," she said as she reached him. "I can't remember the last time."

"One of my specialties." He smiled at her. "To be honest, I'm a bacon addict, so a BLT is one of my fixes."

Rae laughed. "There are worse things to be addicted to." She leaned her hip against the cabinet as she watched him. "Is there anything I can do?"

He shook his head. "Just stand there and look beautiful."

She smiled. "I'll do my best."

Arthur nudged his head under her hand and she absently stroked him. It felt so comfortable being with Bear in his kitchen. Like they'd done this a hundred, or maybe a thousand times before.

Bear finished making the BLTs and they made quick work of eating them at the kitchen table. After they tidied up the kitchen, he pulled out a glass bowl with plastic wrap covering it.

"Is that what I think it is?" Rae pointed to the bowl as he set it down. "Banana pudding with vanilla wafers?"

"You've got it." He pulled off the plastic wrap. "It was my favorite dessert when I was a kid."

"Mine, too." She watched him spoon generous helpings into bowls. "Mom used to make it for Carrie and me for a special treat, like when we got good grades on our report cards."

Rae enthusiastically sat down at the table in front of her pudding. "I'm not waiting long for you."

He laughed as he sat with his bowl. "Is it a race?"

"You can't even keep up with me," she responded with a grin.

After they both had seconds, and they'd cleaned up what dishes they'd used, Bear said, "Would you like a beer or wine cooler?"

"Sounds good." She set down the dishtowel she'd been using to dry the dishes. "What do you have?"

Bear looked into the fridge then glanced over his shoulder at her. "Dark beer as well as a couple of bottles of alcoholic root beer and a citrus wine cooler."

She thought about it a moment. "I'll take the root beer."

He retrieved it along with the domestic dark beer and used a bottle opener to remove the caps. "Glass with ice?"

"I'll drink it straight from the bottle." She accepted the root beer from him and raised her drink.

He clinked his beer against her bottle. "To a great day with a fun lady."

She smiled. "To all your critters and their dad."

Bear cocked his head in the direction of the kitchen entrance. "Come on and we can sit in the family room."

A little voice told Rae she should probably be going home instead of relaxing with alcohol and this sexy man.

She told that little voice to get lost.

CHAPTER 11

"*D*o you mind if I take off my boots?" Rae sat on one end of the couch in the family room and set her root beer on a coaster on the end table. "I'm not used to these things and my feet are killing me."

"Be my guest." He set his beer on the coffee table then knelt on one knee in front of her. "I'll even help you get them off."

"Thank you, kind sir." Rae leaned back on the overstuffed leather couch, sinking into the softness. Maybe she shouldn't be taking off her boots, but she wanted to spend more time with Bear, and she might as well be comfortable.

He grasped the boot heel and sole and tugged, releasing her foot and causing her to let out a sigh of relief. She waited as he pulled her other boot off and she wiggled her toes. "That's sooo much better."

"You need to prop your feet up." He moved onto the couch beside her, slid his arm beneath her knees, and shifted her so that her feet were in his lap. "Now that should feel good."

"It does." She stretched out her toes then relaxed them. "I think it might take a while to get used to those boots."

"If they fit right, shouldn't take too long." He pulled off one sock and then the other and stuck them in one boot. He started massaging one of her feet. "You did a great job today."

"That feels wonderful." She sighed with pleasure. "As far as riding, I've learned a lot from a great teacher."

She wondered what he'd do if she sat in his lap rather than just having her feet propped up on him. She really wanted to find out, but she remained where she was. "Thank you for letting me ride Angel."

He continued massaging her foot. "My pleasure."

"You do that so well." She wriggled on the couch. "Where did you learn it?"

"Picked it up somewhere." He shrugged as he set down her foot and grasped the other one. He glanced at her. "I give great back massages, too."

She held in a grin. "You're in trouble."

He raised an eyebrow. "Trouble?"

She gave an emphatic nod. "I'm going to end up asking for a back massage next."

"I don't mind." He gave her a sexy little smile as he continued massaging her foot. "Means I have an excuse to get my hands on you."

She warmed at the thought of having his hands all over her. She definitely liked that idea.

"You don't need an excuse," she said softly, then wondered where that came from. But then, she knew exactly where.

Her desire for Bear was off the charts.

He rested his arm across her shins and paused, his focus entirely on her. He clearly sensed her desire, or maybe he saw it in her eyes, on her expression.

Bear shifted and gathered her into his arms in an easy movement. She rested her head against his chest and put her hand on his bicep. She listened to his heartbeat, steady, reassuring. He smelled so masculine and of sun-warmed flesh. He felt as solid as a rock, his embrace making her feel safe, secure.

He adjusted her position so that he could look into her eyes. His were dark, sparkling with something she couldn't define. He spoke quietly, yet firmly. "I could fall for you, Rae. Maybe I already have."

Her skin tingled and warmth spread throughout her. She should tell him to let her go and leave. This was moving way too fast—for both of them.

Instead of fleeing, she slipped her hand into his hair and cupped the back of his head and drew him down to her.

His mouth met hers, and he softly explored her lips before sliding his tongue between them. He tasted incredible and she loved the warm sensations he stirred inside her with his kiss.

A moan rose within her and she couldn't hold it back. She returned his kiss with a fervor she'd never felt before. He intensified his kiss, driving her desire to new heights.

She slid her hand beneath his T-shirt so that she could enjoy the feel of his firm body. He felt solid and muscular and she couldn't help but imagine their naked bodies intertwined.

Something in her head told her again that maybe she was pushing things too fast. She pulled her hand away, but he caught it in his.

Instead of trying to stop herself and halt things, she took his hand and placed it on her breast.

Bear groaned as he cupped her breast. He raised his head, breaking the kiss, and looked into her eyes as he traced her nipple with his thumb. "You are so beautiful, Rae."

She sighed with pleasure and arched her back, pressing her breast against his hand, wanting more. She pushed her T-shirt up, moving his hand aside long enough to get her shirt above her bra.

He stared at her breasts, her rosy nipples visible through the lace of her bra. His throat worked and he couldn't seem to tear his gaze away.

She couldn't wait for him. She pulled her bra beneath her breasts. "Suck my nipples, please."

He met her gaze for a long moment then lowered his head. He slipped her nipple into his mouth and gently sucked.

"Bear." Her voice came out loud and urgent as she wriggled in his arms. "That feels so good. Please don't stop."

"I won't, hon." He moved his head to her other nipple, and she whimpered. "You taste like sunshine," he murmured.

She slid her hands into his hair as he sucked her nipples. It wasn't enough. She wanted more from him, she *needed* him.

Rae shifted in his arms and straddled his lap. As he watched, she pulled her T-shirt over her head and tossed it aside. She unfastened her bra and let it fall to the floor.

He seemed mesmerized, staring at her breasts, then raising his head and looking into her eyes. "You are an incredible woman."

She shimmied on his lap, rubbing herself against the hard ridge that told her all she needed to know—he wanted her, too. He groaned and grasped her hips, forcing her to still. "You are driving me crazy."

"Good." She kissed him, hard, daring him to rachet up the intensity.

He moved faster and smoother than she thought a man of his size could. One moment she was straddling his lap and looking down at him. The next moment, she was on her back on the couch, looking up at his gorgeous face.

He eased between her knees, his hips spreading her thighs apart. She wrapped her legs around him, holding him tightly to her.

She squirmed and cried out as he sucked her nipples. He tugged on one with his teeth and a sort of sweet pain burst through her that amplified her desire.

"Bear." His name came out on a gasp. "I need you."

He moved away from her breasts, his hands braced to either

side of her head as he met her gaze. "I need you too, Rae." He lowered his head and nuzzled her ear. "I want you like crazy."

"Then take me." She couldn't believe the words coming out of her mouth. "I'm yours."

He captured her mouth, kissing her with fervent desire.

She wanted to feel his naked flesh against hers and couldn't wait any longer. She pushed his T-shirt up and he helped her pull it over his head.

"You're beautiful." She slid her palm over his smooth, muscular flesh. "So perfect."

Rae met his gaze and he wore that sexy grin that made her melt. "I'm beautiful?" he said in a teasing tone.

"Absolutely." She looped her arms around his neck. "Now kiss me with that gorgeous mouth."

"Yes, ma'am." The look in his eyes took her breath away.

She held on to him, rubbing her naked breasts against his bare chest as he brought his mouth to hers.

It felt so incredibly good with nothing between their bare skin. Rae thought she would lose it if she didn't feel all of him. This man drove everything from her mind but the desire to be with him.

She needed him more than she'd needed anything or anyone before.

Rae clung to Bear like a lifeline, as if he could save her from anything and everything. He was a beacon in a dark, stormy sea, warning her away from the dark and guiding her toward a bright light, drawing her closer and keeping her safe.

He raised his head and their gazes met and held. The man who'd been a little shy and hesitant was gone. A confident man who needed her and wanted her now had taken his place.

Bear rose, straddling her thighs. He watched her as he moved his hands to the button of her jeans and easily unfastened it. She found herself holding her breath as he lowered the zipper.

He eased off the couch and caught her off guard as he scooped her into his arms. She gave a little cry of surprise and flung her arms around his neck as if afraid of falling.

"What are you doing?" she asked as he straightened to his full height.

"Taking you to my bedroom," he said as his big arms held her to him. "Where we'll both be a lot more comfortable."

She smiled. "Carry on, honey bear."

He grinned as he started carrying her away from the family room. "Honey bear?"

She gave an emphatic nod. "You are to me."

"Well, all right then." He reached what she assumed was the back of the house and he carried her into a room and flipped on the lights. The light given off by the lamps on the nightstands was comfortable and not too bright.

He set her on the bed, which was high enough her feet couldn't reach the floor.

"I'd like to take a shower." She smiled up at him as he stood between her thighs. "I could use some help scrubbing my back."

"I'd be happy to offer my assistance." He wore a teasing grin as he took her hands and helped her to her feet.

Rae smiled and pushed her jeans and panties down. She stepped out of them before heading through an archway, through which she'd seen a gray and brown stone-tiled countertop with twin sinks.

She felt Bear's presence behind her as she walked up to a luxurious stone-tiled shower with a huge showerhead.

He turned on the water and when the temperature was right, he ushered her in. Water fell like warm, softly falling rain from the showerhead.

"This is wonderful." She closed her eyes and gave a sigh of pleasure as the water rolled over her head and down her face and arms. "Best shower ever."

Bear stepped in behind her and pressed himself against her.

She widened her eyes in surprise at the feel of his erection against her bare flesh.

He pulled the band out of her hair, setting her hair free.

Rae turned in his arms as water fell over both of them, running over their faces and bodies. He was so handsome with his strong, sun-tanned features and his stubbled cheeks. He kissed her and she closed her eyes, loving the feel of his naked body against hers and the loveliness of his kiss.

He broke the kiss and looked down at her. "I only have my body wash and shampoo. Nothing girly-scented."

She laughed. "I don't mind smelling like you. I love your scent."

He smiled and reached for a bottle of shampoo off a built-in shelf in the rock-tiled wall. He poured a good amount onto his palm and rubbed it into her hair.

She sighed as he massaged her scalp and lathered her hair. He rinsed it out, then used his body wash and a shower scrubby sponge to cleanse her skin. He washed her backside before he moved on downward. He took his time, soaping her shoulders and paying close attention to her breasts. He stopped when he reached her mound then soaped the trimmed hair and the juncture of her thighs. She shivered as her need built with every movement of the scrubby.

Every movement he made was slow and gentle, and incredibly erotic.

Bear knelt and soaped her legs. She braced her palms on his shoulders to steady herself as he soaped each of her feet. His shoulders felt so solid and strong beneath her hands.

When he finished, the big man stood and unhooked a spray nozzle and used the soft spray to wash away the soap bubbles. He gently caressed her skin with the fingertips of one hand as he sprayed her with the nozzle using his other.

When he finished, he put the nozzle back in its holder and faced her. He cupped her face in his hands. "You are so beautiful,

Rae." He ran his thumb along her cheekbone. "You're special to me."

She rested her palms on his heavily muscled pecs and searched his gaze. "You're special to me, too, Bear." She slid her hands up to his shoulders and he lowered his head to kiss her.

When he drew away, she gave him a sensual look. "My turn to wash that big, gorgeous body of yours."

He grinned. "You're going to give me a big head if you keep that up."

"I call it as I see it." She grasped the sponge he had gently scrubbed her with and squirted gel on it from the same bottle he'd used.

She started washing his body, corded with muscle in all the best places. Beneath his lab coat, and with his low-key demeanor, she'd had no idea he was so physically powerful. Once she'd seen him in a T-shirt and jeans, she'd had a good idea. Now, seeing him completely naked, she was floored by this beautiful male specimen.

Rae took her time, enjoying every moment of exploring his body. When she reached his large, rigid erection she got a good look at what was in store for her. Butterflies traveled through her body, just imagining having him inside her.

She used the sponge to wash around his cock and he groaned. His muscles bunched, like he was fighting to get control of his desire.

Water rolled over him, soap running in rivulets down his thighs until it washed away. She knelt on the tile at his feet and looked up at him. He had his palms braced against the tiled wall and he stared down at her. His jaw was tight, and his eyes were dark and stormy with need.

Bear couldn't think straight as he watched Rae now down on her knees. She grasped him in one hand and cupped his balls in her other hand, and his entire body tensed. She slowly lowered her head and her lips slid along his length.

Her warm mouth was heaven. He sucked in his breath, unable to move, mesmerized by the bobbing of her head as he slid through her parted lips…in and out, in and out. He fought to keep his eyes from closing so that he could watch her taking him places he hadn't been to in quite the same way before.

Water ran down his body and cascaded onto Rae. It rolled over her face and down to her gorgeous, perfect breasts with pretty pert nipples. She looked so beautiful, so sexy and perfect as she knelt in front of him.

The desire to climax slammed into him. It built so quickly he didn't think he could stop it from taking over.

"Rae." His voice was rough as her name came out. "I need you."

She let him slip from her mouth and he helped her get to her feet. "I need you, too."

"Let's get to the bedroom." He almost couldn't speak. "I have condoms there."

"Fuck me here." The word on her tongue surprised him. He liked the way it came from her and it made him want her with even more ferocity. "I'm on the Pill."

He clenched his jaw as he picked her up and pressed her against the wall. She gasped at the force he used. Not hard, but not gentle. He could barely control the need raging through him.

She wrapped her thighs around his hips, and he moved the head of his erection to her core.

He couldn't wait. He watched her face as he slid inside her core.

Rae's eyes widened and her lips parted. "Oh. My. God," came out in gasps.

Bear moved in and out, holding her gaze as he took her. He clenched his jaw, fighting not to climax too soon. He wanted to stay in heaven as long as possible.

Her breasts bounced as he increased his pace and her thighs tightened around him. He moved hard and fast now, barely holding back to make sure he wouldn't hurt her. He *needed* her like nothing he could ever have imagined.

"Bear." His name almost sounded like a sob as she spoke it. "I can't wait."

"Hold on, honey." He moved in and out faster. "I'm going to come with you."

"Please, please, please," she begged him over and over.

He growled out the words, "Now, Rae *now*."

Rae screamed his name and he shouted hers. He throbbed inside her as she shuddered around him.

He didn't stop moving. He couldn't stop. The feeling was so exquisite that he wanted it to go on forever.

She shuddered and cried out again, and then it was too much for him. He groaned, his body throbbing from the strength of his climax and the power of their lovemaking.

His knees weakened and he slowly lowered her so that they were both kneeling on the shower's tile floor

His harsh breathing caused his chest to rise and fall. Rae looked like she was having a hard time pulling herself together, too.

He settled on his haunches and dragged her to his lap. She wrapped her thighs around him and clung to him. He held her until strength returned to his limbs.

"Thank you." She spoke the words in her sweet voice. "Thank you, Bear."

He leaned back enough to look in her eyes and the corner of his mouth quirked. "I think that's a mutual feeling." He wrapped her in his arms again. "You are amazing, Rae."

Still holding her, he got to his feet and turned off the water. "Can you stand?"

She nodded against his shoulder. "Yes."

When he set her down, she swayed on her feet and he steadied her. "Are you sure?"

She nodded. "I just needed a moment."

After giving her another moment, he grabbed a thick towel and rubbed it over her body. He towel-dried her hair and let it fall in a mass of tangled locks that made her look like a woodland pixie. She looked sated and entirely contented as she watched him dry himself off.

Bear tossed aside the towel and scooped her into his arms.

She shrieked in surprise and clung to him with a laugh. "You keep doing that."

He grinned. "Just to hear you squeal like that. It's cute."

She lightly punched his shoulder. "You might be bigger than me, but I can kick your butt."

He laughed at that. "I bet you can." He tossed her on the bed, and she cried out again.

She fell into helpless laughter. "I can't catch my breath."

He crawled onto the bed and braced his hands to either side of her head. "Tell me when you do, and I'll make love to you again."

Her laughter died away and she smiled up at him. "Breath caught. Now come to me."

CHAPTER 12

"Stay the night." Bear couldn't stop looking at Rae's beautiful face as he stroked her hair.

She shifted in the bed, adjusting the covers as she faced him. Her smile seemed strained. "Marlee will worry."

"Call her." He held her chin in his fingertips. "Knowing Marlee, she'll be fine."

"I can't." Rae rolled away from him and slid her legs over the side of the bed. She scooped up her panties and jeans and tugged them on.

Bear tried not to frown at her abruptness. They'd shared so much, and he wanted to hold her all night. She meant something to him, a lot to him. Did she feel the same, or had this just been sex to her?

He mentally shook his head. He couldn't believe Rae had only wanted sex from him. He'd seen the way she looked at him, how she smiled at him. She couldn't have faked that—could she? Was he being naïve?

She straightened as he climbed out of bed. She looked so pretty with her hair a mess, wearing only jeans. Her beautiful torso was bare, her incredible breasts on display.

"I—the rest of my clothes are in the family room." She looked nervous, and maybe even close to tears.

This time he did frown, and he moved toward her. "Are you okay, Rae?"

She avoided his gaze, looking instead at her hands. Her voice came out so quiet he could barely hear her. "I just need to go home."

He took her by the shoulders. "Look at me, Rae." When she didn't, he took her face in his hands and moved her so that she had to meet his gaze. "What happened between the time we made love and now?"

Her bottom lip quivered. "There are things you don't know about me." Her throat worked as she stared up at him. "What if you hate me when you find out?" A tear rolled down her cheek, causing his gut to twist.

"Honey." He gently wiped away the tear with his thumb. "Unless you're married, nothing you could say could make me upset with you. Even if you are, I couldn't hate you."

More tears rolled down her cheeks. "I need to get dressed."

"Only if you promise to stay longer." He brushed tears away from both cheeks. "Otherwise I'm going to tie you down until we clear this up. We can't leave things like this."

She closed her eyes, her features filled with pain. She opened them, her eyes still glittering with tears. "I'm not married."

"Are you dying from cancer or something else?" he asked softly. "Is that why you think I'll be upset?"

"No, it's nothing like that." Her throat worked as she swallowed. "Let me get dressed and I'll stay, long enough to tell you everything."

"I'll get some clothes on then we'll get your clothes." He pulled on boxer briefs, a pair of old jeans, and a faded T-shirt as she stared at a bronze cowboy on a bucking bronco that sat on his bureau.

When he was dressed, he offered his hand. She hesitated, then took it.

They reached the living room and he found her bra and T-shirt and handed them to her. She dressed slowly, as if putting off the time of truth as long as she could. She dug in her pocket and drew out another band and pulled her hair back into a ponytail before she plopped on the couch.

His gut clenched as he sat close to her and took her hand. What was she about to tell him?

She cleared her throat and didn't look at him. This time he didn't force her to face him, he simply prepared to listen to whatever it was that had her so torn up.

"Just over a year ago—" Her voice broke and she gathered herself together before starting again. "Some friends rented a houseboat on Lake Powell and we went to a bar, fairly close to my home in Coyote Lake City." She spoke slowly, as if stating facts.

"While we were at the bar, a man kept trying to pick me up." Her face twisted into a scowl. "I made it clear I wasn't interested, and he started calling me things like 'whore,' and other words I won't repeat."

Anger warmed Bear's skin. Rae deserved to be treated like a lady. Every woman did. To hear how this man had verbally abused her made the heat on his skin turn into fire.

"I decided to leave the place and I told my friends I wanted to go back to the houseboat because I'd had enough of men. They tried to convince me to stay, but the man had really gotten under my skin. We'd come in separate cars, so I drove to the houseboat alone."

Bear tensed, afraid he knew what was coming next.

"I was getting ready for bed when I heard a crash." Rae's voice caught. "At first I thought it was my friends, but I didn't hear any conversation and they're usually pretty loud. Then I heard a man call out my name and saying, 'where are you, little bitch?'"

Her throat worked as she swallowed. "I had no idea who it was, and I was terrified."

Bear's heart beat a little faster as he listened to Rae's story.

"I went to call 9-1-1, but I'd left my phone in my car." She shook her head and closed her eyes tight. "That was so stupid. If I'd had it with me, maybe none of this would have happened."

Rae looked so distraught that Bear took her hand and lightly squeezed.

"One thing our grandmother had done was teach us how to shoot and had drilled into us that we should keep a gun with us for protection. I got my little Smith and Wesson out of my purse."

Bear wanted to gather Rae in his arms, but he sensed she didn't want that.

"I heard another crash and I was even more terrified. I hid in the closet right before the bedroom door opened. The light came on and a man shouted, 'Where are you, bitch?' I was so scared I could barely think."

She went on. "I held my gun, but my hands were trembling, and I almost dropped it. I gripped it tighter right before he opened the closet door."

Rae took a deep breath. "It was the man who had harassed me at the bar. He started yelling at me, saying I thought I was too good for him and he was going to teach me a lesson. He said other things, too, that I don't want to repeat."

The rage Bear felt against the man was something he'd never experienced before.

Tears rolled freely down Rae's face. "He dragged me out of the closet by my foot. I struggled and screamed and tried to get away. When he got me in the middle of the bedroom, he stopped and stared down at me. That was when he noticed I had a gun."

Rae looked helpless. "It didn't faze him. He should have been scared. He should have left. But he didn't." Rae started sobbing and Bear gripped his hands into fists. "He lunged for the gun. So many thoughts went through my mind. I thought if I wounded him, it would stop him long enough for me to get away and call the police."

Her face was red as she cried and told her story. "But he fell on me and the gun went off and shot him in the belly. I don't know if I intentionally pulled the trigger, or the motion forced the movement." Her shoulders shook. "Ultimately, it didn't matter. He collapsed and I managed to get him off of me. There was so much blood and he was screaming in pain and rage. I ran for my phone in the car and called 9-1-1."

She shook her head as she continued. "I was covered in his blood. I didn't want to go back into the room. I still had the gun, so he couldn't take it if he was even able to get up. But I was afraid he'd die." Her voice cracked. "I didn't mean to kill him."

Rae looked at Bear, her eyes wide and begging for something, maybe forgiveness for what she'd done. As far as he was concerned, there was nothing to forgive.

Bear gathered Rae into his arms. "Shhh."

"I didn't mean to kill him," she repeated as she sobbed against his T-shirt. "I didn't mean to kill a man."

Bear started rocking her. "You were protecting yourself. The bastard could have killed you."

"I was eventually arrested and charged." She buried her face against his chest. "I'm going to trial for manslaughter."

Bear's skin prickled. "You're being prosecuted?"

"You wouldn't believe the hell I've been through since meeting that man at the bar. Public attacks in the media and online, signs in my front yard, and messages in my mailbox. Even death threats." She clenched her fist in his shirt. "The prosecutor thinks she can prove that I invited that-that bastard to the houseboat. Basically, that I'd asked for it."

Bear squeezed her tighter to him. "I'm so sorry, honey. I'm so sorry you're going through this."

She turned her face to look at him. "You don't think I'm a terrible person for killing a man?"

He studied her red, blotchy face. "How could I think that? You're a wonderful person who doesn't deserve to be going through this." He took one of her hands in his. "How could you believe that I would think any less of you?"

She swallowed. "After what I've been through, I'm afraid everyone hates me. I lost my home, my career. I've left behind what friends and family I have to get away from it all the best I can." It looked like she had something else to say, but then she sagged against him.

"You have friends and family who care about you," Bear said. "*I* care about you."

"I'm so tired of it all, Bear," she said. "The trial is in a couple of weeks. I'm so afraid I'll end up going to prison just for defending myself."

The thought of Rae going to prison was like a knife through his gut. He wrapped both arms around her as he tried to control the feelings going through him. "Do you have a good lawyer?"

"Very good." She sighed. "I've sunk a lot of my savings on my defense."

He pressed his lips against the top of her head. "Just know you have me now. I'm not going to let you go through this alone."

"I can't ask that of you." Her voice was quieter now. "You barely know me."

"It's like I've known you all my life, Rae." Bear stroked her hair. "You're a part of me now."

"Thank you." Her voice was barely above a whisper. "Thank you for being you."

Bear's mind tried to grasp the enormity of what Rae had been through. How could anyone make it through what she had unscathed? It wasn't possible.

"Spend the night with me." He spoke the words quietly but firmly. "You shouldn't be alone right now."

She was quiet a long moment. Finally, she said, "I need to call Marlee and let her know."

Relief poured through Bear that Rae had agreed. He didn't like the idea of her dealing with this alone right now and leaving this way. As a matter of fact, he didn't intend to let her go through any of this ordeal alone anymore.

RAE TRIED to pull herself together. She'd just lost it in front of Bear and had chosen an awful time to do it. They'd shared such a beautiful day and night together, and she'd let loose what was ugly and wrong in her life afterward.

He'd taken it in a way she hadn't expected. He'd comforted her and told her that he wasn't going to let her go through this alone. She didn't know exactly what he'd meant, but it was good to have his support.

She padded barefoot to the kitchen, where she'd left her purse, and dug her phone out. She went to her favorites list and hit speed dial for Marlee.

Rae stared at the doorway to the kitchen as she waited for her cousin to answer. The kitchen was dark, and she jumped when something scampered across the floor. She let out a breath of relief when she realized it was one of his cats. Maggie, she thought.

"Hi, Rae." Marlee's voice came on the line. "Everything okay?"

"Everything is fine." Rae felt like a schoolgirl calling her mom and making up a story that she was staying with a friend instead of her boyfriend. "Did I wake you?"

"You know me. I stay up late to work on my crazy quilts." Marlee sounded like she had a smile in her voice. "So, what's up?"

Rae hesitated. "I'm going to spend the night at Bear's."

A pause and then a soft laugh. "I had a feeling about you two."

Rae's face heated. "It's been nice. Make that a terrific day." She added to herself, *Most of it.*

"And a fabulous night?" Marlee said in a teasing tone.

"Fabulous," Rae said with a smile. She didn't clarify to Marlee that the good parts were what had been so wonderful. "I'll let you go since you have something sporty to do in the morning."

"I might have a tennis match with Cherie at seven. She's going to call early and let me know." Marlee yawned. "Guess I should get to bed."

"Thanks, Marlee," Rae said quietly. "You've always been there for me and you don't know how much I appreciate it."

"I would do anything for you," Marlee said. "You know that."

"I do." Rae's voice grew more intent. "And you know I'd move mountains for you, too."

"We are a mutual appreciation society," Marlee said, a smile in her voice. "Love you, cuz. Enjoy your night."

"Love you." Rae disconnected and blew out her breath. She looked up and saw Bear in the doorway, his hands shoved in his front pockets.

"Everything okay?" He moved toward her as she dropped the phone in her purse. "You took so long, I started to worry you'd left."

"I would never leave without telling you," Rae said solemnly. "Promise."

He reached her and wrapped her in his big arms. "Need to talk about anything else?"

She thought about her intention to move to New Mexico when this was all over, but it seemed so far away. Could she change her mind and stay in King Creek?

But would she be forever tainted by what had happened?

"No, I've told you everything that I can think of that's important about what happened." She pressed her face against his chest, breathing in the scent of his T-shirt that smelled freshly laundered.

"We can go to bed." He rubbed her back. "Unless cherry pie is involved in staying up a little while longer?"

She couldn't help a grin as she tilted her face to look at him. "You know the way to my heart."

"If that's all it takes," he matched her grin, "I've got it made."

Bear heated the pie in the microwave and topped each slice with a mound of vanilla ice cream. In no time they were seated with bowls and spoons, and glasses of ice water.

"Best bedtime snack ever," Rae announced after she'd eaten a bite of warm pie and ice cream. The treat was also making her feel better after her hard cry. "Dessert always helps the world go 'round a little better."

Bear smiled. "I hear you." He reached over and placed his hand over hers. "I'm glad you're staying the night."

"I am, too." Warmth flowed through her in a warm wave. "When do you have to leave for the clinic?"

"I don't go into the clinic on Mondays unless there's an emergency." He slid his fork under a portion of the pie. "My tech sets up my appointments at ranches around King Creek and I examine and treat livestock."

"Are you leaving early for your first appointment?" she asked.

He swallowed the bite of ice cream he'd just eaten. "I don't leave until 7:30." He pointed his fork at her. "But you don't have to leave that early. You can stay as late as you want."

"I'll leave when you do." She grasped her glass of water. "I need to do laundry. I was a bad girl and didn't get it done Saturday."

They continued chatting, like she hadn't just poured out her harsh reality. It was comforting being with Bear, and she wanted to spend every moment she could with him.

After they finished and cleaned up what little mess they'd made, Bear took her hand and led her to the bedroom. He gave her a T-shirt to wear to bed, rather than expecting her to wear nothing.

When they slipped beneath the covers, Bear spooned Rae, but she found she wanted him more than ever. She turned in his arms to face him and traced her fingers along his jaw line.

He studied her, his eyes soft and caring. She kissed him slowly at first, then passion took over. It was like every pent-up feeling took over and she needed him in ways she could never have explained.

Bear seemed to try to slow her down at first, but he got caught up in the intensity of her desire. They made love with fierce passion that drove her to new heights. Afterward, as she spiraled down from the peak, Rae found herself exhausted.

He kissed her gently, then proceeded to make love to her sensually, making her body and senses alive yet again. He took her to the clouds at the same time he kept her grounded.

This time when Rae climaxed, her entire body shuddered, and she went limp. Bear groaned with his own release, then gathered her into his arms so that they were lying face to face.

She'd never felt so protected, so cared for, and maybe even loved. How had she been so fortunate to meet a man like Bear? Did she deserve to feel the intense happiness that she was experiencing at this very moment?

Bear pressed a kiss to her forehead, his lips firm. "Sleep, hon."

Rae smiled and closed her eyes, drifting off within moments to a peaceful sleep.

CHAPTER 13

Rae drove back to Marlee's home after enjoying breakfast with Bear. She pulled up to the cute cottage-style house at the same time her cousin came jogging around the corner. By the time Rae was out of her car, Marlee stood on the sidewalk, waiting.

"I'd hug you, but I'm too sweaty after my run." Perspiration rolled down the side of Marlee's face.

"I take it your tennis date with Cherie fell through," Rae said.

Marlee nodded. "So, a jog it was instead." She propped her hands on her hips as she smiled. "Well?"

Rae couldn't help a smile of her own. "Let's get out of the heat and get something to drink."

"Smart girl." Marlee glanced up at the crystal-blue sky. "No rain in the forecast, but maybe we'll get lucky this afternoon, anyway."

Rae opened the white picket fence gate then walked with Marlee up the short sidewalk to the porch. Marlee slipped a key out of a hidden pocket in the waistband of her jogging shorts and opened the door.

Cool air flowed over them as they walked into the bright interior. Marlee loved sunshine and opened up all the drapes in the morning to fill the house with sunlight. In the kitchen, Marlee pulled a jug of water out of the fridge, poured two glasses, and handed one to Rae.

They clinked glasses. "Cheers," they said before downing their drinks.

After drinking a considerable amount of water, Marlee inclined her head toward the hallway. "I'll take a quick shower, then we'll sit down and have girl-talk."

Rae opened the fridge and pulled out a cold jar. "I'll pour the iced coffee."

Marlee took off, leaving Rae to her thoughts. Her belly flip-flopped at the memory of her night with Bear.

So much emotion had been wrapped up in a matter of hours. She had loved her time with him throughout the day and their lovemaking had been wonderful. Unfortunately, she had fallen apart, but still, Bear had accepted her explanation and stated he would be with her throughout the rest of the ordeal.

But was that fair to him?

When Marlee returned, her long hair was still damp from the shower, wetting the shoulders of her T-shirt. She pulled up a chair at the whimsically painted table that she had picked up at a consignment shop.

Rae handed Marlee a glass of iced coffee and sat across the table from her cousin with her own drink.

Marlee took a sip then planted her elbows on the table, her face in her hands. "Well, start already."

Rae folded her arms on the table and leaned forward. "Bear is an amazing man." She couldn't help a smile. "He's sweet, sexy, thoughtful, kind, caring—"

"And the list goes on." Marlee laughed. "I grew up with the man and his brothers, so you're not telling me anything new." Her smile turned to a wicked grin. "What I don't know, is how the hot vet is in bed."

Heat rushed to Rae's cheeks. "Pretty amazing."

Marlee made a move forward motion with her hand. "Go on."

Rae thought about what to tell her cousin. "He's sweet and attentive but can be incredibly passionate and intense."

"Ooooh." Marlee's eyes sparkled. "I'm liking this story."

Rae couldn't help a laugh. "Beneath that lab coat, you'd never dream he could have such an incredibly hot body. He looks great in anything, like a T-shirt and jeans, but naked—O.M.G."

Marlee sighed. "Total envy over here. Absolutely green with it."

Rae tipped her head to the side. "You are the light shade of new grass."

"I'm surprised I'm not the color of a pine tree." Marlee braced her chin on just one hand. "What else?"

Rae thought about the night, all the good parts. "He's got this power about him. Strong, able to do anything."

Marlee nodded. "Like leaping tall buildings in a single bound."

Rae grinned. "That too."

"What's he like in the, um…" Marlee looked like she was thinking of how to say it best. "He's got big hands and feet, so does that translate to other parts?"

Rae figured she was probably bright red by now. "Uh-huh."

Marlee sighed again. "One of these days, maybe I'll get so lucky."

"Bear does have two unmarried brothers," Rae said.

Marlee rolled her eyes. "Brady is a year older than Bear, but he's still too young, 'cause I like men older than me. Colt—let's just say he and I have *never* gotten along."

"Why not?" Rae asked. "He seems nice enough."

Marlee waved away the question. "A story for another day." She braced her forearms on the table and leaned forward. "I want to hear more about Bear."

"He's a nice package all the way around." Rae pulled her braid over her shoulder and played with the end. "I sort of fell apart at one point, though."

Marlee frowned. "Why?"

Rae drew in a deep breath. "After the world's greatest sex, and realizing what an amazing man he is, I felt like I was unworthy."

"What?" Marlee straightened. "Why in the world would you feel like that?"

"The whole shooting and killing someone thing." Rae gripped the end of her braid. "I felt like I was tainting Bear and he didn't deserve that."

"That's bull, Rae." Marlee's frown deepened. "So, what happened?"

"He saw I was upset," Rae said quietly. "And he wouldn't let me go until I explained why." She paused a moment. "I told him everything."

Marlee studied Rae. "How did that go?"

"Like you'd expect when it comes to Bear McLeod." Rae gave a little smile. "He listened, believed me, and was supportive. He said I'm not going to go through this alone, that he's going to be with me through it all."

Marlee smiled. "I'd expect nothing less from Bear."

"Don't you think it's too soon for Bear to promise to go through this with me?" Rae asked. "I haven't known him very long."

"For some people, you feel like you've known them forever." Marlee looked thoughtful. "From what I know of Bear, he doesn't do anything lightly. And he's got pretty good judgment. Except when it came to Jennifer Mayfair."

"Who's that?" Rae cocked her head to the side.

"His ex-girlfriend." Marlee made a face. "She hadn't lived here long when they started dating, and I guess she did a good job of pulling the wool over his eyes."

Rae was afraid to ask, but did anyway, "What happened?"

"Bear wouldn't talk about it," Marlee said. "But word had it that she cheated on him with a cowboy who couldn't keep his mouth shut if you paid him half the gold in Fort Knox."

"I can't imagine what he went through." Rae's heart hurt for Bear, even though she was grateful he wasn't with that woman now. "He didn't deserve that."

"No, he didn't." Marlee shook her head. "Jennifer has been getting around since Bear broke it off with her. Guess we all know now the kind of woman she is."

"What do you think I should do?" Rae asked. "About Bear promising me he's going through this ordeal with me?"

"Bear is a smart man," Marlee said. "When he's serious about something—or someone—he's all in. From what I can see, he's all in when it comes to you. I think you should consider what he's offering. You can't get a better man on your side than Bear."

Rae slowly nodded. "I believe that's true, and it would be wonderful to have him there, on my side. I just don't know that it's fair to him."

"Let him decide that for himself," Marlee said. "You've given him the facts, which is good. Now he'll have to figure out how far that support goes. He might just give you emotional support when he's with you, or he might want to do something more. You'll just have to see."

Rae drummed her fingers on the tabletop for a moment as she thought about the week ahead. "Bear asked me last week to go to the Fourth of July celebration with him."

Marlee perked up. "I'm going with some girlfriends. I'd planned to invite you but looks like you'll be having more fun than we will."

"It does sound great," Rae said. "He told me a little about it."

Marlee took a long sip of her iced coffee before setting it down. "Fourth of July is a big deal around here."

Rae sobered drastically and she slumped in her seat. "I can't help but be afraid that after next week, this could be the last fun I'll have if I'm convicted."

"*No.*" Marlee narrowed her brows. "No way will you be going to prison."

Rae tried to turn her thoughts to a positive outcome. "It's hard, Marlee. I know that I'm in the right, even though I didn't mean to kill him. But I'm still scared."

Marlee put her hand over Rae's. "I refuse to believe anything but the fact you'll be coming back home after the trial. No other outcome is possible."

Rae gave her cousin a weak smile. "Thanks for believing in me."

Marlee gripped her hand tighter. "Always."

"I have a week's worth of laundry to do." Rae straightened in her seat. "Are you working today?"

"I feel like I'm always working." Marlee blew out a puff of air that raised the now dry bangs that were long enough to flop into her eyes. "The joys of working from home."

"Got a big project?" Rae asked.

Marlee nodded. "A huge edit for a guy who thinks a thousand-page book is what readers want."

Rae held up her fingers in the warding-off sign. "Better you than me."

"Hmph." Marlee stretched her arms above her head. "Speaking of the tragedy I'm about to edit, it's time to get into my office."

Rae scooted back her chair as Marlee did the same. Rae picked up her iced coffee and downed it. "I'm not going anywhere today that I know of, so holler if you need me for anything."

"Will do." Marlee hugged Rae. "I'm here for you, Rae. Hang in there and it will all be over soon, and you can marry Bear McLeod and live in King Creek."

Rae sputtered with laughter. "You are too much."

Marlee gave her a cheeky grin. "Just sayin'."

Rae shook her head as her cousin left the room. Marlee was

just teasing, but the thought would have been a nice one if she didn't think she'd end up having to leave the state.

COLT'S RANCH was Bear's last stop of the day. Colt had a mare with an infection on her foreleg and Bear gave his brother an ointment to treat the wound. He watched as Colt applied the ointment to the mare in her stall.

Bear had done his best to avoid being distracted during the day while he made his rounds of the ranches on his schedule, but frequently his thoughts turned to Rae. The passion they had shared had been amazing in ways he never dreamed of, and images from their night filled his head more often than not.

However, he couldn't help but think about what she'd told him about the break-in and her trial. He couldn't believe she'd end up going to prison—the thought was inconceivable. What she must have been going through all these months would be more than most could take.

"What's going on in that brain of yours?" Colt asked, jarring Bear out of his thoughts. "Not like you to be daydreaming."

Bear rubbed his temples. "Just got some things on my mind."

Colt came out of the mare's stall and latched the gate. He hitched his shoulder up against a post and folded his arms across his chest. "What's eating you?"

Bear frowned, not sure he wanted to explain everything to Colt. But the way his brother was looking at him, he knew he was going to have to say something.

"Got a cold one in the fridge?" Bear asked.

Colt pushed away from the post. "You bet."

They headed to the house and Colt didn't press Bear to talk until they had their beers and were sitting on the back patio, overlooking the pool. It was still hotter than hell, so Colt turned on the misters he'd had installed a couple of years ago that were common in the Valley of the Sun. Bear had something similar on his own back porch.

They kicked back on the patio furniture. For a long moment, neither man said a word, Colt clearly waiting for Bear to get it out.

"Rae stayed the night." Bear couldn't help a smile at the memory.

"Hot damn." Colt slugged Bear's shoulder. "Way to go little brother."

Bear rubbed his arm. Colt had a hell of a punch. "I care for Rae a lot, Colt. She's going through some things that most men couldn't handle."

"Like what?" Colt took a pull on his beer bottle.

"She's on trial for murder." The words came out before Bear even knew he was going to say them.

Colt's stunned features said it all. "What the hell?"

Bear braced his forearms on his thighs, his beer in one hand, and he stared at the tiled patio floor. He bypassed the part about their making love and went straight to everything Rae had told him about the bastard who'd verbally assaulted her and later broke into her home.

When he finished, he looked at Colt. "She goes on trial next week."

Colt blew out his breath. "Hell of a thing to spring on a man."

Bear stared at his bottle. "She's pretty torn up about it. Can you imagine wondering if you're spending your last days as a free man before you go into the courthouse?"

"No, I can't." Colt spoke in a sober tone. "Where are you going from this point?"

Bear looked at his brother. "I'm going to see her through this. I know she's going to beat the charges. She just needs the support of family and friends."

"Do you count yourself as a friend?" Colt asked.

"More than a friend." Bear stared out at the pool, the crystal-clear water still as glass.

"Of course, she'd have Marlee on her side," Colt said. "Anyone else?"

Bear lowered the bottle he held and faced Colt. "One sister. Rest of her family has passed on."

"Friends?" Colt asked.

"I'm not sure." Bear thought about Rae's face as she told him everything, and the memory tore at his gut. "But one thing I do know is that I'm going to be there."

Colt turned his gaze toward the pool. "From what I know of her, which isn't a lot, I tend to agree with you that she's going to come out of this standing. My gut says the same thing." He looked back at Bear. "For what it's worth, she has my support."

"That's worth a hell of a lot." Bear killed his beer with another swallow. "Are you going to the Fourth of July celebration with anyone?"

Colt shrugged. "Tex Arnold asked me over to a barbeque with him and the family and a few friends. Knowing him, that means half of King Creek."

Bear grinned. "I got an invite from his wife."

"You going?" Colt asked.

"Might," Bear said. "I'm taking Rae to the celebration, so we might go to Tex's for dinner and then off to see the fireworks."

"Sounds like a good plan." Colt finished off his beer and raised the empty. "Ready for another?"

Bear thought about having to get up early for work in the morning but figured another beer with his brother wouldn't be a bad idea. "Sure." Bear smiled at Colt. "One more and then I've got to get home."

"And call your woman," Colt replied with a grin.

Bear liked the thought of Rae being "his woman," then wondered what she'd think about that term. It worked both ways—he'd be her man. "Yeah." He smiled. "And call my woman."

. . .

When Bear got back to his ranch, and after he took care of the animals, he went into his home office and powered up his laptop. He started to do an Internet search on Rae, then hesitated.

He trusted Rae, but was he being blinded by what he felt for her? Would researching what had happened be a sign he didn't trust her?

The more he thought about it, the more it seemed like a good idea to look into what had happened. Not that he didn't trust her, but he needed more information to support her, information she might not have thought to tell him.

He put her name in the search bar, along with "Coyote Lake City" and got immediate hits. He studied images that popped up with the results, and his chest hurt for her when he saw her mug shot. She looked tired and afraid. She wasn't redheaded in the photo, but blonde. When he'd met her, it had been easy to see that the red wasn't her natural color, but it still jarred him to see her as a blonde.

A professional photo was on the image of a business card, stating she was a real estate agent. Bartending was a long way from her old career, but he imagined it would be difficult to keep clients when one was charged with murder.

He turned his attention to articles dating back to when the story first broke. The anger he felt was so strong it surprised him when he read about what the man had done to Rae and how resulting actions had changed her life. It worsened as he scanned over social media attacks and several news articles slanted against her.

Bear continued on. He didn't see much more than she'd already told him, just more details. When he finished reading what he'd found, he sat back in his chair, his elbow on the armrest as he stroked his chin.

Rae had been through a hell of a lot, and now her freedom

was at stake. He told her he'd be at her side, and that's exactly where he intended to be when she walked into the courtroom.

CHAPTER 14

Red, white, and blue banners fluttered in the breeze as Rae and Bear walked down King Creek's cordoned off Main Street. Music filled the air along with laughter and chatter and she smiled at the Fourth of July festive feeling in the air.

A wonderful week had passed since their picnic, wonderful because of the time she'd spent with Bear.

A whistle came from one end of the street and he gripped her hand. "The parade is about to start."

Rae looked in the direction the whistle had come from but didn't see anything. Bear led her to the sidewalk, and they stood along the street with the crowd. He gripped her hand and smiled down at her.

She looked into his eyes and marveled at the caring she saw in the depths. After all she'd told him, and he'd accepted it without judging her or looking at her any differently.

Someone's shoulder slammed into Rae and she stumbled forward. Bear caught her arm, or she would have tumbled into the street.

She looked up to see a gorgeous brunette standing in front of her. "I didn't see you standing there." The taller woman spoke with an English accent as she looked down at Rae. She didn't apologize and turned her gaze on Bear.

Rae tried not to frown as the woman sidled in between Rae and Bear, her back to Rae.

"Bear, love." The woman rested her hand on Bear's arm. "I haven't seen you for a couple of weeks."

Bear's expression remained neutral as he gently removed the woman's hand and his tone was polite as he said, "Hello, Jennifer."

This must be the English woman that Marlee had told her about, the one who had cheated on Bear.

Bear and Rae seemed to be of the same mind as they reached for each other's hand. Bear shifted so that they were standing together again, Jennifer in front of them.

"Jennifer, this is Rae." Bear gave a nod to Rae as he gripped her hand tighter. "Rae, this is Jennifer."

Rae moved closer to Bear, so that she pressed against his biceps. Rae did her best to keep her tone light. "Hi."

"Haven't I seen you somewhere before?" Jennifer's brown eyes had a malicious gleam to them as she raked her gaze over Rae. "Oh, yes. You were in the papers in Phoenix. You killed your lover in Coyote Lake City."

Fire burned up Rae's neck to her face and she couldn't get a word out.

"Rae and I are going to watch the parade now." Bear's eyes had a hard glint to them, an almost dangerous look that Rae would never have associated with him. "Have a good day, Jennifer."

He gripped Rae's hand and drew her along with him, closer to where the whistle had come from.

The backs of Rae's eyes stung. She wanted to scream and cry and slap that woman's face. Instead, she let Bear take her to another spot on the parade route.

Marching band music started up as they stood on the

crowded sidewalk. She glanced up at Bear, hoping he didn't believe the man she'd killed had been her lover. She wanted to tell him that, but she didn't know how to say it, or that she even should in the current situation. He probably couldn't have heard her anyway. Did he believe Jennifer?

Bear released her hand and slid his arm around her shoulders. He leaned down and murmured in her ear. "I'm sorry about Jennifer. She shouldn't have said that."

Rae exhaled with relief and leaned into Bear. She needed his strength and his support.

An older model convertible appeared around the curve of Main Street, the flags mounted on each side snapping in the breeze. The crowd cheered as the lead car crawled forward and a marching band followed. Majorettes carried a banner in front of the band that read, *King Creek High School*.

The tension that had filled Rae slowly seeped away as she let herself enjoy the parade. She wasn't going to let a witch like Jennifer ruin her day with Bear.

A baton twirling team followed the band, then next came a float decorated with red, white, and blue streamers and rosettes. A *Miss King Creek* banner was draped along the side of the float, and a young woman perched on a throne wore a sash with the same proclamation across her torso.

Another convertible came by, this one a modern luxury car with a *Re-elect Mayor Brown* sign on the door, a white-haired man waving from the passenger seat. A pair of clowns rode tiny bikes in circles behind the mayor's car, the clowns throwing wrapped candies toward children along the crowded sidewalk.

The festive feeling in the air had Rae smiling, and she waved back at the children riding the next float. Several floats went by and more convertibles with political party banners.

The parade was surprisingly long for a small town, and Rae found her spirit buoyed by the cheers and laughter around her. She clapped and cheered with the crowd as the parade went on and she ate a piece of candy that Bear caught and handed to her.

The last float had passed by, followed by the final convertible, and Rae turned and grinned up at Bear. "I've never had so much fun at a parade. There's something about being in a small town with an event filled with locals to make it more enjoyable than a production put on by a large city."

Bear draped his arm around her shoulders and smiled. "I've always thought so." He released her long enough to take her hand and walk toward a lot filled with vendors. "Hungry for lunch?"

"Famished." Rae pointed ahead to the row of food trucks. "The burger that man over there just bought looks massive." She tilted her head to smile up at Bear. "Perfect."

He gave her a teasing smile. "That burger is bigger than you are."

She grinned. "Yeah, but I'm up to the challenge."

He laughed and they strolled over to the food truck.

Two huge burgers and large Cokes later, Bear and Rae made their way to the game stalls and dunk tank.

At the dunk tank, Bear gestured to the man climbing the steps up to the seat above a tank of water. "We made it just in time to see Mayor Brown dunked." He looked at Rae. "All the proceeds go to a local children's charity."

Rae recognized the man she'd seen in one of the convertibles in the parade. The man, who had to be in his seventies, had wispy white hair and black-framed coke-bottle glasses. He sat on the platform and waved at the crowd, which broke into a cheer.

"The way everyone is cheering, he must be popular." Rae ran her gaze over the crowd. "I noticed his re-election sign on his convertible."

"He's well-liked." Bear rested his hand on her shoulder. "He was known as a sort of prankster before he was elected, and he keeps the rest of the politicians on their toes. When it comes down to it, no one can keep up with the mayor."

"He sounds like a good guy." Rae watched people line up with softballs they had purchased to throw at the lever, which would drop the mayor's seat and dunk him when struck.

"He is," Bear said. "I treat his livestock and pets." He tugged Rae's hand. "Come on. You can show me your pitching arm."

Rae laughed. "What pitching arm?"

They stood in line to purchase the use of softballs to try to dunk Mayor Brown. Rae watched as young men and women waited their turns.

First up was a boy of about ten, who missed with all three of his pitches. A girl who couldn't have been older than eight, came up behind him and missed each time, too. Next, a cowboy took his turn, but failed to dunk the mayor.

A young woman of about sixteen threw her first ball with a fast, underhand pitch that told Rae she had to be a pitcher on softball team. The ball struck the lever and the mayor dropped into the tank.

The crowd cheered as Mayor Brown came up sputtering and laughing. He gave the young woman a thumbs up and she grinned. Bear explained that the rules stated the participant got to dunk the mayor once and had to surrender any additional balls. The girl gave back her two remaining balls and it was the next person's turn.

"Doesn't he get tired?" Rae shook her head as the mayor climbed up the ladder two more times before it was hers and Bear's turn to throw.

Bear shrugged. "I would."

Rae shook her head and smiled. "I doubt that."

She threw the three balls Bear had gotten for her and missed each time. Bear missed his first try, but nailed the lever on the second, sending Mayor Brown back in the drink. The crowd cheered once again, this time with someone crying out, "Way to go, Doc McLeod."

Bear and Rae moved on to watch the pie eating contest, with

about twenty men and women sitting at a line of picnic tables, each in front of a pie and each wearing a large plastic bib. "That's my brother, Brady, next to Colt." Bear pointed to a good-looking man who resembled him and Colt.

A woman announced the pie eating contest and thanked the Parent-Teacher Organization for donating the pies. She gave the names of each contestant and Rae thought the cheers for the McLeod brothers were the loudest.

After a donation can went around the crowd, Miss King Creek held her hand over a button on a large three-minute timer. The men and women at the picnic tables remained poised, hands tied behind their backs, in front of their pies. A judge blew a whistle and the young woman slammed her hand down on the timer's button.

The contestants dove face-first into the pies, which turned out to be cherry. Red coated their faces. The timer counted down as laughter and cheers came from the crowd. Before the timer reached zero, two men straightened, their pie plates mostly clean. One of the men was Colt, and the other she didn't recognize. Rae thought Colt's looked the cleanest of the two, but from her angle, she couldn't be certain. The timer's horn blew and everyone else stopped.

Colt's and the other contestants' faces were covered in cherry pie filling. Colt and Brady were laughing and talking to each other as their hands were untied. The judges conferred and then the one with the whistle stood.

"The winner is Colt McLeod," the judge announced.

The crowd cheered. Face still coated with cherry pie, Colt stood up and raised his hands like a champion prize fighter before he was awarded a trophy topped with a gold pie. The contestants got up and hosed-off their faces as the volunteers prepared the area for the hotdog eating contest.

Bill Porter won the next contest. Rae didn't mind him so

much now that he had started behaving thanks to Bear. She congratulated Bill before Bear guided her over to Colt and Brady.

Colt gave her a big hug when she congratulated him, and Bear introduced her to Brady.

"Good to meet you." Brady shook her hand. He had a firm grip, like his brothers. "Colt mentioned you two might be stopping by Tex Arnold's for dinner."

Rae glanced up at Bear, who nodded. "Tex and his family are having a barbeque tonight," Bear said. "We can go if you like."

"Sure." Rae smiled. She turned back to Brady. "Looks like we'll be there. Will you?"

Brady nodded. "So's the rest of the clan, as far as I know."

"I guess we'll see you then," she told Brady with a smile. At the same time, she felt a major pang of nervousness. *The rest of the clan?* She gulped. She was not ready for that.

Bear and Rae moved on, enjoying more festival activities. Bear bought homemade fudge from a small vendor, and shared it with Rae as they walked around Main Street.

LATER IN THE AFTERNOON, Bear slipped his arm around Rae's shoulders, enjoying the feel of her close to him. "Are you ready to go to Tex's for the barbeque?"

She nodded. "I'm getting hungry again."

First thing, they picked up three dozen assorted cookies from Rachel's Bakery to take to the barbeque. Once they had a dessert to contribute, they walked to Bear's truck, which was parked at the southern end of Main Street. He set the cookies on the floorboard of the back of the truck's cab.

He helped Rae into his vehicle, then made his way to the driver's side and climbed behind the wheel. In moments, he was driving toward his friend's ranch.

"I have a feeling you'll like Tex and his wife." Bear guided his truck onto the two-lane highway, then looked at Rae. "They have several kids, too. Fun bunch."

"I'm sure I'll like them." She smiled. "They're your friends, so they have to be nice."

He turned his attention fully on the road. "What did you think of the festival?"

She sounded enthusiastic. "I don't think I've ever had so much fun at any festival I've been to in Coyote Lake City." He glanced at her again and saw that her eyes were sparkling. "Thank you for taking me."

He smiled. "There's something to be said about small towns."

Rae shifted in her seat. "I never knew what small towns were like until I moved here."

He focused on the road. "And your conclusion?"

"So far, so good."

He figured he'd take that as a positive.

His mind churned over the confrontation with Jennifer. He had no doubt her statement had been malicious, designed to hurt Rae and give him doubts. He didn't doubt Rae, but he wondered if his judgment was off, like it had been with Jennifer.

Bear gritted his teeth. He trusted Rae, and his Internet search had made it clear she'd told him everything she could. He had only her word of her innocence, but her word was enough, as far as he was concerned.

He exited the highway and took a left at the second intersection he came to. "We're almost there."

"I'm nervous, Bear." She wore an expression filled with uncertainty when he glanced at her. "I have avoided private gatherings, especially big ones, in case someone recognizes me from the papers." She looked at her hands in her lap. "Like the woman from the festival."

"Don't let Jennifer's comment bother you." He reached over and put his hand on hers as he glanced to the road and back to her. "I'll stay with you every second tonight, and if you want to leave, we'll leave."

She didn't say anything as he looked back to the road. When she spoke, her voice was low. "I'm sure everything will be okay. I want you to know that I appreciate you more than you can imagine."

"I care for you, Rae." His voice felt thick as he spoke. "I'm not going to allow anyone to make you feel anything but welcome."

She squeezed his hand in return, but he felt the tension through their physical connection.

Bear took the dirt road to the Circle A, Tex and Linda Arnold's ranch, crossed over a cattle guard, pulled up to the main house, and parked next to several other vehicles.

"This place is huge." Rae looked around at the multiple buildings that surrounded Tex's home.

"He has a good-sized cattle operation, one of the biggest in the county," Bear said. "His ranch is about the same size as my brother, Carter's. Colt's ranch is nearly as big."

"It looks like Tex invited half of King Creek." Rae met Bear's gaze. "There are a lot of cars here."

Bear gave her a gentle smile. "Are you ready?"

She gave a firm nod. "As I'll ever be."

He got out, shut the door, and strode to the passenger side. He helped Rae out of the truck before getting the box of cookies.

The sound of laughter and chatter came from behind the ranch house. Rae gripped his hand tightly as they walked around Tex and Linda's large home to the expansive lawn in the back.

Friends and neighbors stood or lounged around the lawn and swimming pool. A group of kids played tag football. Several adults and teens swam or played volleyball in the pool.

Rae tensed, likely surprised and overwhelmed by the number of people she saw when they reached the backyard. "There are more people here than I'd guessed," she said, confirming his thoughts.

He gently nudged her. "Come on, hon. I'll introduce you to Tex and his wife."

Rae gripped his hand and took a deep breath before letting it out. "Let's go."

He guided her to where Tex stood next to Brady, both men holding a can of beer.

"'Bout time you got here, Doc." Tex grinned and shook his hand.

"I'd like to introduce you to Rae Fox, who moved here not too long ago from Coyote Lake City." Bear inclined his head in Rae's direction. "Rae, this is Tex Arnold."

"A real pleasure." Tex gripped Rae's hand.

She smiled. "Your place is amazing." Tex released her hand and she looked to Brady. "Looks like you got all that cherry pie off your face."

He grinned and touched the brim of his Stetson. "Came close to Colt and Davie, but Colt took it."

"I hadn't heard that," Tex said. "Didn't you win last year?"

"Yep." Brady nodded. "Just couldn't cut it today."

"Where's that beautiful wife of yours?" Bear asked Tex. "I don't see Linda."

"There she is." Tex looked in the direction of the brunette opening the patio door, carrying a dish with a domed lid. "Looks like she might need help." Tex hurried up to Linda and took the dish from her.

She rubbed her hands on her jeans as she leaned close to Tex. She drew back and turned to see Bear and Rae.

"Hi, Bear." Linda smiled and came toward them. She hugged Bear then held her hand out to Rae. "You must be Rae. Welcome to the Circle A."

"Thank you." Rae took her hand for a moment before releasing it. "I love your home."

"Thanks for inviting us," Bear said to Tex and Linda. "Where would you like us to put this? We brought a few dozen cookies."

"Right over there." Linda pointed to a table covered in desserts. "If you can find a spot."

"Will do." Bear took Rae's hand again. "I see some family that I need to introduce to Rae."

Tex gave a nod and Linda smiled. Bear could feel Rae's apprehension through their linked hands as they walked to the dessert table. He released her long enough to set the box on the table and lift the lid.

When he finished, he escorted her toward several of his family members, and hoped Rae wasn't feeling too overwhelmed.

Justin and Miranda stood closest and Bear took Rae toward them.

"Hey, bro." Justin rested his hand on Bear's shoulder before smiling at Rae.

Bear introduced Rae to Justin and his fiancée, Miranda, and explained that Rae moved to the town fairly recently.

"Welcome to King Creek," Justin gripped Rae's hand then released it. "How do you like the town?"

"It's great." Rae smiled. "I had a ball at the festival today. You can't find anything that feels quite like it in a bigger town, or in a city."

"I came to the area from Texas, not too long ago. I loved it from the moment I arrived." Miranda pushed hair behind her ear. "What do you do?"

Rae hesitated. "I was in real estate in Coyote Lake City. When I moved here, I decided to take a low-key job at Mickey's."

"What do you think of working for the big guy?" Justin asked.

"Mickey is a good man." Rae looked like she genuinely meant it. "And he's a great boss."

"Does Patty give you a hard time?" Justin asked. "If she does, don't let it bother you—her bark is worse than her bite."

Rae shrugged. "We've come to an understanding."

"How did you two meet?" Miranda asked Bear and Rae.

Bear explained about Rae bringing in Arthur after he'd been hit by a car.

"Then he showed up at Mickey's that night," Rae said. "We just clicked."

Bear rested his hand on Rae's shoulder and smiled. "Something like that."

"How did you and Justin get together?" Rae asked Miranda.

"I'm a horse therapist." Miranda looked at Justin and back to Rae. "Justin's daughter, Kaycee, was thrown from a horse and developed a fear of riding. I helped her through it."

"Miranda works magic," Justin said, and Miranda smiled.

Bear nodded in the direction his and Justin's oldest brother stood. "I'm going to introduce Rae to Carter and Kit."

"It's great meeting you," Miranda said. "I'm sure we'll see you around."

Rae smiled. "I'm sure you will."

Justin touched the brim of his hat and nodded to Rae.

Bear guided Rae toward Carter. "You've met Colt, Brady, and Justin. Carter is the oldest of the McLeod bunch."

Rae glanced up at him. "Your brothers and you are all so tall. I feel really short next to you and them. Miranda is tall, too."

Bear released his hand and rested his arm around her shoulders and drew her close. "You're absolutely perfect."

They reached Carter, who was talking with Brady.

Brady stepped back as Bear introduced Carter to Rae. After Carter greeted Rae, Bear asked, "Is Kit around?"

Carter inclined his head toward a group of their family standing near the pool. "She's with Mom and Grandma. Looks like Jill, Leann, and Haylee are there, too."

Bear caught a glimpse of his pretty sister-in-law, who had hair the color of butterscotch. "I see her." He nodded to Carter and Brady before drawing Rae away. "And you can also meet more of our family," Bear added.

Rae fell into step beside them, but she looked nervous. Bear took her hand again and squeezed. She looked up at him, took a deep breath, and smiled. He loved that smile like crazy. It did things to his gut that he'd never felt before.

When they reached the group, Bear introduced Rae to his mom, Julie, and Grandma Francis; sisters Jill, Leann, and Haylee; and sister-in-law, Kit. The women greeted Rae as if she were a dear friend, rather than an outsider. Bear couldn't help but feel proud of the women in his family, and proud of the wonderful woman Rae was.

Bear's future sister-in-law Miranda joined them, and the seven women drew Rae into conversation, laughing and chatting as they asked how she liked King Creek and about her life in Coyote Lake City. Rae was understandably evasive about some questions but did talk about her sister and her former occupation.

Rae, in turn, asked his family questions about their lives. He could tell her nervousness had faded some, but she still had a hard time letting go of her reservations. Not that he could blame her, after all she'd been through.

Bear stayed with Rae, even though he was the only male of the group. He didn't want to abandon Rae when she had only just met the women in his family.

When Rae started to look a little tired, he realized it had been a long day and she might be hungry.

"Okay, ladies." He cut into the chatter with a smile. "I'm going to introduce Rae to Dad and Grandpa now, and then get us some food. It's been a while since we've had anything to eat."

After they departed, Rae met his gaze. "I am loving your family. They are all so nice."

"I happen to agree." Bear inclined his head in the direction of the two men they were headed toward. "Last two introductions and then we'll grab something to eat. Sound good to you?"

Rae nodded. "Perfect."

Bear's Grandpa Daniel liked to tease, and he made Rae laugh.

Bear's dad, Joe, was good-natured and friendly to Rae, too. She seemed relaxed with the men, even more so than she had been with the women. He imagined it was because there were only two men at this moment, as opposed to the group of six women.

Bear told his dad and grandpa he was going to get Rae something to eat. As he drew her away, Rae seemed tired.

"I guess meeting that many people in one day must be exhausting," he said as they walked to the end of the line at the food tables.

She gave him a smile. "A little. I like all of your family. Your brothers are great and everyone else is, too. There are just so many of them that it is a little overwhelming."

"I can imagine," he said. "I grew up in a huge family, but sometimes it can be a bit much for me, too. I need my quiet time."

"I'm not surprised." She smiled. "You're probably the quietest of the bunch."

"I am." He nodded. "But I wouldn't give them up for anything."

"If they were my family, I wouldn't want to give them up, either." She looked ahead to the food table. "The hamburgers and fudge we ate seem like a long time ago." She craned her neck to see the other table. "And those desserts—I want to try one of each. My eyes are definitely bigger than my stomach."

He chuckled. "Why not go ahead and do your best?"

She grinned up at him. "I might do just that."

Rae did a good job of finishing off a pulled-pork sandwich and sides, plus a piece of chocolate cake and a couple of cookies. He did his fair share of lightening the tables of some of their loads, too.

After they ate, they made their goodbyes and headed out to his truck. It was getting dark, and soon it would be nearing the time the fireworks would be set off. Rae rested her head against his arm as they walked to his truck. "Thanks for bringing me," she said.

"Are you up for watching the fireworks?" he asked. "Or are you ready to go home?"

She smiled up at him. "I wouldn't miss the fireworks for anything. But then home is a really good idea."

They drove to a spot in King Creek, where they could watch and get a good look at the fireworks show that was one of the best in the county. He parked in the lot next to other vehicles, and like other people gathered there, he pulled out a couple of lawn chairs for them to sit in. While they watched the display, Rae looked delighted.

"I've never seen better fireworks," she said when it was over, and they were settled back in his truck.

"I'm glad you enjoyed it." He smiled at her. "It's been a long day, and I bet you're tired."

She covered a yawn and nodded. "I am going to crawl in bed and sleep 'til noon."

Bear rested his hand on her thigh and smiled. He tried not to imagine how beautiful she would look in his bed right now, naked.

He swallowed. "Thanks for spending the day with me."

She smiled and put her hand over his. "I had a great time. I'm really glad you asked me to join you."

He gave her thigh a light squeeze before slipping his hand into her hair and kissing her. The kiss was long, slow, and sweet.

Bear drew back and looked into her eyes. "If you weren't tired, I'd take you home and make love to you all night."

"I'm not that tired." Her breath seemed to quicken. "As a matter of fact, I'm not tired at all now."

His chest grew warm. "Then how about we go and make some fireworks of our own?"

She gave him a sexy smile. "Let's go."

CHAPTER 15

Several weeks after her fantastic Fourth of July with Bear, and many more wonderful times with him, Rae found herself inside the courtroom, wondering if the past months in King Creek had been her last as a free woman.

Next to her sat her attorney, Luther Deming, who studied his notes. Across the aisle from him sat the prosecutor, a hard-looking woman with a confident demeanor, who honestly scared the hell out of Rae.

Bear had intended to be here today, but she had flat out insisted he couldn't come and demanded he respect her wishes. She refused for his last memory of her to be seeing her in handcuffs, being taken away to prison.

He had argued, but in the end, he had respected her desires and said he would wait for her phone call. He'd clearly been upset, but watching her walk away in chains, if it came to that, was unacceptable

Carrie and Marlee, however, sat behind her. Both her sister and her cousin could not in any way be dissuaded to stay home. They were her family and had been with her every step of this horrible ordeal. Bear was important to her, but this was different.

Rae tried to swallow down her fear. This could become the worst day of her life. Losing her freedom would be far worse than everything that had happened to this date.

And it would mean she'd lose Bear, someone she'd come to love.

Love. What an awful time to admit to herself that she was in love with the wonderful man, who had changed her life.

Tears stung at the backs of her eyes. Her hands shook and she rubbed her palms on her thighs, over the tailored suit skirt.

She couldn't allow herself to give in to the despair that hovered on the edge of her mind. Over and over she told herself that she *would* be found innocent and she would *not* go to prison.

Luther leaned close to her. "Hang in there, Rae. You have nothing to worry about. It is going to be tough going through this, but in the end, I am positive you will be found innocent." He gave her a fatherly look. "It'll be okay."

She tried to nod but she felt frozen, her entire body stiff now.

The command to rise for the judge's entrance caused a jolt to go through her. This was real. It was happening now.

Luther touched her elbow and guided her to stand. Somehow, she got to her feet without collapsing back into her chair.

Everything blurred, and Rae thought she might pass out. But once the judge was seated, she sank back into her chair and waited for the next moment and the next, the minutes and hours spent that would determine her fate.

∽

THE TRIAL LASTED ALMOST three full days, but the jury came back with the verdict in an hour.

Which terrified Rae. Either the twelve jurors had all agreed she was guilty, or all agreed she was innocent within no time at all.

Rae felt as if she'd been to hell and back as she stood next to her attorney to learn her fate.

Her ears buzzed as the verdict was announced and she was afraid she hadn't heard right.

Not guilty.

She'd been found innocent of all charges.

The judge stated she was free to go and slammed down his gavel.

Rae heard Carrie sob with relief and the loud exhale Marlee made, as if every moment spent in the courtroom had left her unable to breathe until now.

Luther helped Rae to her feet as the courtroom broke into loud conversations. "You did good, Rae. Congratulations."

She turned and hugged him, tears spilling down her cheeks. "Thanks, Luther. Thanks for saving my life."

He patted her on the shoulder, and she stepped back, brushing tears from her eyes with the backs of her hands.

In the next moments, she was hugging Carrie and Marlee, their tears mingling with their conversations. They intended to go to Carrie's house and have a celebratory dinner accompanied by wine, and lots of it. Rae planned to call Bear with the news, so that he wouldn't worry any more, and she could share her relief with him.

In the hallway outside the courtroom, Larry's family and friends glared daggers at her and she knew they would never believe she was innocent.

She swallowed down the pain and anger that rose inside her. She didn't deserve this, but she'd have to live with it for the rest of her life.

Rae, Carrie, and Marlee made their way outside. Rae was immediately assaulted by reporters. Locals bearing signs with *Murderer* emblazoned across them screamed at her. The horror of the last year and now this assault, threatened to cause her to lose control. She wanted to shout for everyone to leave her alone, to stop throwing accusations her way despite the verdict in her favor.

She had been found innocent by a jury of her peers—yet in people's minds, they would still wonder if she was guilty, or would believe she absolutely was guilty, and that she had somehow gotten away with murder.

Could she stay in King Creek? Was it far enough from Coyote Lake City that she would be away from all the hatred and evil that was the only thing left for her here?

∽

RAE HADN'T REACHED out to Bear after the "not guilty" verdict. She hadn't been able to get herself to make that call.

Instead, after the trial was over, Marlee had made the call to Bear for her, despite protesting that Rae should be the one. She'd heard her cousin make excuses for her, telling Bear that Rae wasn't feeling well and was exhausted from the ordeal.

All of that was true, but more than that kept her from talking with Bear.

Her heart couldn't take it. She was in love with him.

More than she wanted to admit.

More than she could allow herself to feel.

When they'd arrived at Carrie's home, two signs had been staked on her sister's lawn. *Rae Fox got away with murder*, the signs read.

Rae had thrown up on the grass.

Even Carrie's world had been tainted by what had happened to Rae.

Marlee and Carrie had been beyond pissed and took the signs down and threw them in a nearby construction dumpster. Rae sprayed her sick off the lawn with a hose while she felt like she had been crushed, a ten-ton weight resting on her chest.

Rick, Carrie's husband, had the news on when they walked

through the door. A reporter attacked her with barbed questions in a clip, insinuating she had gotten off when she shouldn't have. The anchor went on to say that social media had blown up with accusations that she was a murderer who'd gone free.

Carrie had asked Rick to turn off the news. He did so immediately and apologized—he hadn't realized they were home. He was a good guy, and Rae knew he'd never want to hurt her.

But after all of this, even New Mexico was far too close.

King Creek seemed like another lifetime ago.

Maybe she'd go somewhere big, where she could get lost in the crowds and just be another human being in an ocean of beings. New York City or L.A. seemed to be the best candidates for total absorption of her life.

Both cities were expensive places to live, but she could cash out her investments and stock portfolio as needed, and she'd be okay for a while, at least long enough to get settled and find a job. Maybe she could get back into real estate.

But could her heart take it if she left Bear?

Carrie and Marlee had tried to get Rae to celebrate her freedom tonight, but the best she'd been able to do was drink the wine they handed her. She was grateful to be free, but it felt like the whole situation was far from over. If she stayed around, it would only last longer. Even people in King Creek had probably heard of the trial and connected it to Rae.

All the wonderful people she'd met, and the new friends she'd made, must think less of her now. She could imagine the small-town gossip mill would be at full strength.

She rubbed her forehead with her fingertips, her head aching.

Marlee curled her feet under her as they sat together in the living room with their glasses of wine. The kids were in bed and Rick had gone up to his study.

"What are you thinking, Rae?" Marlee asked, drawing Rae out of her thoughts.

Rae shifted on the couch and stared at her wine glass. "I need to move out of state, but Albuquerque is too close. Maybe New York City."

"Are you serious?" Carrie's eyes widened. "After you've built a new life in King Creek?"

"I thought you changed your mind." Marlee looked at her with astonishment. "You really would leave everything you have behind?"

"What do I have?" Rae struggled to keep her voice steady. "I have you two and my nieces. Otherwise, I have people who hate me and won't ever forget what happened and won't ever stop blaming me." She waved her hand toward the front of the house, as if she could see the signs still posted there. "I'm Rae Fox, murderer, according to them."

"The horrible people who left those signs shouldn't be allowed to dictate your future," Carrie said.

"You have King Creek to go back to," Marlee said quietly. "You have Bear."

A lump stuck in Rae's throat as she fought not to cry. "I should never have developed a relationship with him. I can't let him be with me when this horrible ordeal is now stuck to me like a stain. I will never get away from it all."

"King Creek is small and far enough away that no one from here will be able to hurt you," Carrie said.

"You've made a lot of friends since you moved in with me," Marlee added. "People love you there."

Rae squeezed her eyes shut as she considered what her cousin and sister had to say. Her voice cracked. "Three hours isn't far enough from this place."

"Don't make any decisions today." Marlee moved to the couch on one side of Rae. "You've had a rough time, to put it mildly, and you need to allow yourself time to think things through."

Carrie sat on Rae's other side. "Marlee's right. You have a lot going for you in King Creek and with Bear. Don't throw that away."

"Group hug," Marlee said and Carrie echoed her as they hugged Rae.

Rae tried to smile as two of the most important people in her life hugged her. It was so hard to feel any happiness with all that had happened with the trial. Yes, she was free now. But she had a lot shackling her at the same time.

Bear had become one of the most important people in her life and living without him would make her beyond heartsick.

Rae hugged her sister and cousin back, squeezing them tight. She was a lucky woman. She had her freedom, Carrie, and Marlee.

She would do as they asked and not make any decisions at this very moment. But she didn't think her mind would change.

Tainting Bear's life was the last thing she wanted to do.

~

RAE HAD JUST FINISHED breakfast with her family when the doorbell chimed. Her stomach clenched as she imagined finding news reporters on the doorstep, or hateful people here to verbally attack her again.

"I'll be right back." Carrie left the kitchen to answer the door.

After a minute or so, she returned, looking pleased. "Someone's here to see you, Rae."

Rae startled. It couldn't be bad, or Carrie wouldn't be almost cheerful. Before Rae could ask her sister who it was, Carrie left the kitchen again.

Rae followed, feeling nauseated. She walked into the living room, where Carrie was talking with a big man wearing a cowboy hat.

Her heart stuttered as the man raised his head, his eyes meeting hers.

Bear.

Carrie backed away and Rae was barely aware of her sister leaving the room.

Rae fought to keep from running to him and throwing herself into his arms. "What are you doing here?"

Bear moved closer, so that they were mere inches apart. "I'm taking you home."

She found herself shaking her head. "I don't have a home. I was just staying with my cousin. Right now, I don't have a home anywhere."

"You have a home in King Creek." His words were firm, a steely glint in his eyes that she'd never seen in him before. "You have family and friends who care about you. You have me."

"I'm moving to New York City." She blurted out the words. "I need to get as far away as I can from this place, and King Creek isn't far enough."

His expression didn't change. He took her by the upper arms and gripped her firmly, as if that could make her stay. "Let's go home, Rae. We'll talk about this more."

"No." Teardrops rolled down her cheeks. "I can't face all of those people." She pleaded with him. "I can't even face you."

He moved his hands to her face and cupped it while wiping tears from her cheeks with his thumbs. He lowered his head and brushed his lips over hers.

Rae went stock-still, unable to move. But Bear didn't stop. He moved his mouth over hers, gently prodding her, encouraging her to respond. She fought to keep from melting into his arms, but she wasn't strong enough.

She sank against him as he wrapped his arms around her. His kiss remained gentle, as if knowing that was what she needed right now. She sighed softly into his mouth and he captured the sound.

When he raised his head, she didn't think she could breathe anymore, much less think straight.

"Let's go home." He stroked her hair. "Where you belong."

"I came with Marlee," she said.

"I can drive home alone." Marlee's voice came from behind her. "You can ride with Bear."

Rae looked over her shoulder at Marlee, who smiled. "Bear will take care of you."

"Always," Bear said, drawing her attention back to him.

"I'll ride back with you," Rae said. "But I'm not making any promises about not moving away."

He caressed her cheek as he pushed hair away from her face. "One step at a time, hon. We're not rushing into anything, and that includes you leaving."

Rae packed her suitcase and Bear took it from her when she reached the top of the stairs. She watched his big back as he walked through the door, out to his truck.

She turned to face Carrie and Marlee, who stood just feet away.

"Did you two ask Bear to come?"

Carrie shook her head and Marlee said, "No, but he did ask for Carrie's address and I texted it to him."

"You should have told me that," Rae said.

Marlee tipped her head to the side. "Would you have told him not to come?"

Rae sighed. "I know you both want the best for me." She hugged Carrie, then Marlee. "But this is my life and I need to make my own decisions."

"Just make sure your head is on straight when you do," Marlee said.

Rae nodded. But how could she do that while being around Bear?

"Thanks for everything, you two." She swallowed down the lump in her throat as Bear returned. "Thanks for being there every step of the way."

"Of course," Carrie said. "We're family."

"I'll see you at home," Marlee said. "Let me know what's going on."

Rae walked with Bear to his truck and climbed into the passenger seat when he opened the door. She strapped on her seatbelt and waited for him to start up the vehicle. She held up her hand in a little wave to her cousin and sister, who stood on the lawn, watching her go.

Bear didn't ask her about the trial for two-thirds of the three-hour drive, and she was grateful for that. Instead, he talked about his animals, his practice, and his family, keeping the conversation positive.

When he did raise the subject, he said, "Do you want to talk about it?"

He didn't have to say what "it" was.

She shook her head. "I want to put it all as far back behind me as I can." Her throat ached as she added, "Which is why I need to move."

Bear was silent a moment. "Give yourself some time," he finally said.

She looked out the window and didn't answer.

When they reached King Creek, Bear continued through the town and reached Marlee's neighborhood. Cars lined the normally quiet street. Must be a party at the home of one of Marlee's neighbors. It was Saturday, after all.

She was grateful it was so quiet at Marlee's house. Her car was parked in the driveway. She wondered when Marlee would get home. Knowing her, she probably thought Rae needed some time with Bear.

She dug out her key, but Bear took it from her and opened the door.

"Welcome home!" The shouted cheer startled Rae, and she took a step back and stared at the room filled with people. A big banner hung along one wall that read, *"We love you, Rae!"*

Rae tried to make sense of all the people in her cousin's home.

She was hugged by so many people that she was too stunned to respond to their greetings.

It seemed that all of Bear's family was there as well as Mickey, Jane, and even Patty from work, and other people she'd gotten to know since moving to King Creek. The mayor, of all people, was also in Marlee's living room, and Rae had never actually met him.

Someone pressed a wine glass into her hand, and she saw that it was Bear's mom, Julie. "Welcome home, sweetheart."

"Thank you," Rae managed to get out.

"A toast to Rae." Colt caught her attention and she looked at him. "One of the newest members of the King Creek family."

Cheers went up from the people around her, who shouted, "To Rae."

Dumfounded, she looked at Bear. "Did you…"

"No. It was Marlee's doing." He gave her a soft smile. "Everyone is here because they love you."

Marlee squeezed through the crowd and moved to Rae. "I almost didn't make it here before you did. I'd hoped you didn't see me zipping down the highway past you and Bear."

With a soft smile, Marlee rested her hand on Rae's arm. "You know the night I came home, the day before the verdict? So many people had seen the news and told me they were praying for you. I wanted you to see that people here care about you and don't see you any differently than they did before. They're happy things went the right way for you."

Rae swallowed and fought back tears. "Thank you. I think."

"Believe me when I tell you that there was nothing but support in this town for you, every day of the trial." Bear rested his arm around her shoulders. "I hope you see that you belong here."

She tipped her head to meet his gaze. "I don't even know what to think."

He kissed her soundly, then smiled. "I believe you know. You belong here."

CHAPTER 16

Ten months after the trial, Rae and Bear perched on a rock formation on the side of a streambed in the Superstitions. Rae threw pebbles in the creek that was swollen from yesterday's monsoon rain. The air smelled of rich earth, pine, and rain-washed air.

Rae felt like a changed woman. Her life had made a sharp turn for the better and she couldn't imagine being anywhere but King Creek, and with anyone but Bear McLeod. The acceptance by the people of the town, including Bear's family, had been utterly amazing. She felt blessed and that she had a rich life and a future.

Her hair was blonde again, and Bear seemed to like the look. In all ways, she felt like herself again. Actually, better than her old self.

Bear shifted on the rock beside her and she looked at him. He looked lost in thought, and she wondered what was on his mind. The silence between them was comfortable, and the sounds of birds in the trees covered up the quiet.

Arthur sniffed along the streambed, clearly enjoying being up in the mountains with them. He'd turned out to be great with all of Bear's animals, and since they couldn't find a family he belonged to, Bear had adopted him.

Rae tipped her head back and looked up at flashes of sky she saw through the waving tree branches. She definitely had a good life now.

Within days of the trial, Rae's story had been lost in the sea of much bigger news stories on the national level, then on the state level. The furor on social media died down over the next month, and since she was away from Coyote Lake City, she didn't have to face anyone who had a problem with her.

She still lived with Marlee but spent most of her time with Bear. She had considered buying her own home, and she probably should, soon. After all, she'd been living with her cousin for over a year now. Marlee had insisted she loved having Rae live with her, but it really had been too long.

"What's on your mind?" Bear's deep voice broke into Rae's thoughts.

She lowered her head and met his gaze. "I was just thinking it's time to buy my own place. I've been living with Marlee long enough that I'm probably cramping her style."

Bear gave her his sexy grin and she sighed. Life couldn't get much better than sitting next to this man who meant everything to her.

He whistled to Arthur, who loped toward them. Bear rubbed the dog behind his ears and said something low to him that she couldn't hear.

Bear raised his head. "Looks like Arthur's got something on his collar."

Rae reached up and stroked the side of Arthur's neck. "I don't see anything."

Bear cocked his head to the side, watching her. "Check again."

She looked closer and caught a glimpse of red—a ribbon. "How did that get there?" She reached up and touched the length of satin and found that it was tied to his collar. A tiny white envelope was attached to the ribbon. She pulled it toward her and read the familiar scrawl that just managed to fill the space on the envelope.

Special Delivery for Rae Fox.

She glanced at Bear. "What are you up to?"

He shrugged. "Might help you in finding your new home."

Brow furrowed, she pulled the end of the ribbon and it came free from Arthur's collar. The dog looked at her, panting happily, as she caught the envelope.

She shook her head and looked at Bear. "This is supposed to help me find a new home?"

He gave a slow nod. "Yep."

Arthur laid down beside her and rested his head on her thigh. His look said that he was in on it—whatever *it* was.

Bear had such a mischievous grin that it made her grin, too. The tiny envelope was white and thick, something small and hard inside it. She broke the seal and dumped the contents onto her palm.

For a moment she stared at a beautiful ring. A large diamond winked in the flashes of sunlight, and the gold felt cool against her skin.

Rae couldn't process what she was seeing. A ring? An engagement ring?

She met Bear's gaze and he raised a brow. "Give you any ideas on where you can live?"

Her throat worked. "Are you..."

He captured her hands in his, and she gripped the ring, tightly.

"I love you, Rae, more than anything. Yes, I'm asking you to marry me." He opened her hand and took the ring from her. "Will you?"

"Yes." She threw her arms around him, trying not to cry from joy. "I love you, Bear. My honey bear."

Bear drew back and smiled as he took her hand and slid the ring onto her finger. "Guess you'd better start packing."

With a smile just as big as his, Rae raised her hand and studied the solitaire. "I guess I'd better."

Arthur wiggled his way between them, insisting on attention.

Rae laughed. "He's just making sure we remember who brought us together in the first place."

Bear rested his arm around Rae's shoulders as he stroked the dog's silken head. "Don't worry, boy. You can be the ring bearer."

Arthur barked once and Rae smiled at Bear. He kissed her, sweet and gentle, before drawing her closer to his side, letting her know that they belonged with each other—for keeps.

EXCERPT: COUNTRY RAIN

CHAPTER 1

Despite the chill in the late October air, perspiration rolled down the side of Marlee Fox's face as she finished her morning jog. She slowed her pace then came to an easy walk when she reached the sidewalk leading into her neighborhood.

Usually, it didn't start to get to this fairly low temperature for the area until November in King Creek, which was not too far from the metro Phoenix area. This year fall decided to bless them with cooler temperatures. Marlee didn't mind one darn bit.

She drew a breath in and blew it out as her heart rate lowered. She loved the neighborhood she lived in on the outskirts of King Creek. Not quite country and not quite in town—the perfect space to breathe.

"Hey there." Amy Baker waved from her porch.

Marlee came to a stop and smiled at her favorite neighbor. "We haven't done lunch in a while."

Amy's footsteps thunked on the wooden porch steps as she made her way down to the path that led to the sidewalk. "I'm ready for some hole-in-the-wall tacos."

Marlee rested her hands on the split rail fence. "Ricardo's next Wednesday at one?"

"Perfect. I get off work from Heidi's at twelve-thirty. Amy's long brunette ponytail bounced as she nodded. "We haven't had a good gab in what seems like forever."

Marlee couldn't help a grin. "Yeah, two weeks is an eternity."

"Only two weeks?" Amy returned her smile. "Have you heard about the fund-raising event in November to help small businesses in King Creek?"

"I heard someone mention it at Mickey's the other night." Marlee tilted her head to the side. "But I was on my out the door with Ben and didn't hear the details."

Amy raised her brows. "You were out with Ben Campbell?"

"I just ran into him there and we left at the same time." Marlee brushed away the incident with a wave of her hand. Last thing she wanted to get around town was a relationship between her and Ben. "Now tell me about the event."

"With the economy sucking right now, Mayor Brown said he'd like to see something done to help our local businesses." Amy swiped a strand of hair that whipped into her face as a breeze picked up. "I volunteered to help at the event, and I'm doing some recruiting. I know how you like to get involved in the community."

"I'd love to give a hand." The breeze caused Marlee to shiver as the perspiration dried on her skin. "Do you have the details?"

"I never had a doubt I could count on you." Amy smiled. "We can go over deets Wednesday at lunch."

"You're on." Marlee shoved her hands into the pockets of her sweat jacket. "So, where's it being held?"

"The Bar M," Amy said. "Colt volunteered his ranch."

Marlee held back a groan as her enthusiasm deflated, and she tried not to show her sudden reluctance. Amy had no idea just how much she would prefer to *not* be around Colt McLeod. High school had been a long time ago, but she'd never forgotten days better left behind.

She usually managed to avoid Colt. Hard to do in a town full of McLeods, of which her cousin Rae could now be counted amongst.

The ringing of her phone saved Marlee from having to try to find a way to back out of her new commitment. She fished her phone out of the side pocket of her leggings. The screen showed *Rae McLeod*.

"It's my cousin." Marlee raised her phone. "I'd better get this."

"I'll see you Wednesday." Amy gave her a little wave. "Tell Rae hello for me."

"I will." Marlee returned her wave then answered her phone as she walked away from Amy's fence. "Hey, cuz."

"Are you free for dinner tonight?" Rae sounded breathless with excitement.

"You bet." Marlee's calendar was filling up for the week. "What's going on?"

"We can snag our booth at Gus's and I'll tell you over garbage pizza."

Marlee laughed. "Since when did you like your pizza with everything on it?"

"Just hungry for it." Marlee heard the shrug in Rae's voice. "Seven good for you?"

"I'm single, I have no kids, and I live alone," Marlee said. "What do you think?"

Rae laughed. "See you then."

Marlee pocketed her phone and walked the rest of the way home. She frowned as a thought occurred to her. Did Rae's plan for dinner have anything to do with the event at Colt's? She mentally shook her head. Nah. Rae knew that Colt was not Marlee's favorite person, so why would she think Marlee would get excited? Rae wouldn't, so it had to be something else.

The wind picked up as Marlee reached her home and she shivered. She'd have to wear a jacket tonight.

Marlee pushed opened the gate of her white picket fence and jogged up the stairs to the front porch of her ninety-year-old home. The house creaked, wind howled through the windows, the wood floors squeaked, and she wouldn't trade it for anything.

She'd put up Halloween decorations for the holiday and had a witch costume ready for trick-or-treaters who'd be stopping by on Saturday. She had a great neighborhood with lots of kids, so she always had a big plastic cauldron full of candy each year.

After she let herself in, she dropped the key into a dish on a small table and locked the door behind her. She never felt like she needed to secure her door in her small town, but that was only the naïve side of her that wanted to think she was surrounded by good people and didn't have to worry about crime like their not-so-far Phoenix neighbors had. Sure, King Creek didn't have much of a crime rate, but it always paid to be safe.

Marlee's shoes squeaked on the ceramic tiled floor as she made her way to her small kitchen with its whimsically painted table and mismatched yet matching chairs. She'd fallen in love with the set when she spotted in King Creek Treasures, the local consignment store. She'd been delighted to learn a local artist had painted it.

She grabbed a water bottle from the fridge that was covered in magnets from places she'd visited and holding down postcards that friends and family had sent. She twisted off the cap and took long swallows of water before staring at the fridge. One day she wanted to have children and have her refrigerator covered with their pictures and their drawings.

First, she needed a hell of a man for a father. She tilted her head to the side. She couldn't imagine Ben Campbell as someone she'd want a long-term relationship with, much less seeing him as dad material.

For some darn reason, Colt McLeod came to mind, and she

ground her teeth. No way on earth would she have anything to do with him any farther than she could throw him—which would be about one inch if she could even budge that tall, muscular body.

Marlee groaned and tilted her head to look up at her ceiling. She'd had it raised and added crown moldings. She rather liked how it made her small kitchen look bigger and more open.

She lowered her head and blew out her breath. There, did she manage to vanquish thoughts of Colt from her mind? Must be the fact that Amy had told her about the event at Colt's ranch. Time to get that man out of her mind. She pictured him falling flat on his ass in a huge mud puddle in a pig pen.

Marlee couldn't help a laugh. He *so* deserved that.

Maybe she should get a puppy. She scrunched her nose as she gave the thought serious consideration. Bear McLeod, also known as Doc McLeod, was the local vet and her cousin's husband. She didn't hold it against Bear that Colt was his brother. Bear would know what shelters she should look into, or he might even know of a dog that needed a good home.

She downed the rest of her water bottle and tossed the plastic into the recycle bin. She continued to think about bringing a dog into her home as she headed up the squeaking wood steps to the second floor. She'd put off getting a pet for years, but really, why wait any longer? She worked from home as an editor, so the dog wouldn't be alone unless she went out for a while and couldn't take it with her. She had time to train a pet and even take it on her daily jog.

"I'll talk with Rae about it tonight." Marlee tugged off her athletic wear and tossed it all into the clothes hamper.

Enthusiasm buoyed her steps as she headed for the shower. Kids weren't in her near future, but she'd decided a fur-baby was.

. . .

MARLEE LEANED back in her recliner, rubbed the bridge of her nose, and squeezed her eyes shut. She'd been going through the slush pile, looking for a gem of a memoir that would jump and say, "Ta-da! I'm the manuscript you've always dreamed of receiving!"

Ha. Not even close.

Finding a manuscript that completely excited her hadn't happened in a while. Most submissions for memoirs were boring as hell—no one wanted to read about the average person's life. She lowered her hand, opened her eyes, and sighed.

Tomorrow she'd look at her other submissions. She accepted non-fiction queries for parenting, health, biographies, cooking, writing, humor, history, and sports. And thanks to her senior editor, Molly Shoemaker, she now accepted memoirs, currently the bane of Marlee's life.

"Time to pack it up." She rubbed the head of the polished ironwood duck on her end table, the only pet she'd had since she was a kid. "Did I ever tell you I *really* hate memoirs?"

The duck didn't answer.

Marlee intended to go out and have fun with Rae. She needed tonight—red wine and pizza. And she'd even get to eat garbage pizza instead of pepperoni for a change.

She dressed in jeans, a lightweight V-necked black sweater, and athletic shoes, and pulled her blonde hair up into a high ponytail. A touch of makeup and she was ready to go. Who knew if she'd meet the father of her 2.4 children?

Colt once again popped into her brain.

She thumped her skull with the flat of her hand. She'd gotten the man out of her system way back when. So why was he intruding now?

Nope. She was having none of it.

The walk to Gus's Pizza took all of fifteen minutes. The evening was clear and cool, but she wore her purple Phoenix Suns jacket, which warded off the chill.

EXCERPT: COUNTRY RAIN

Warm air flowed over her face as she walked into Gus's. The stained-glass lights over dark-wood booths with red vinyl-covered bench seats gave off a warm glow. The juke box played a country tune by the Phoenix-born son Dierks Bentley.

She looked in the direction of the booth she usually shared with Rae, and her cousin waved her over. Marlee smiled at Rae as she headed across the tiled floor to the booth. Rae looked flushed and happy as she grinned in return.

Marlee slid into the booth and shrugged out of her jacket. "You look fantastic, even more than usual."

"You're good for my ego." Rae laughed. "Best cousin ever." She pointed to the two red plastic tumblers on the table, a straw sticking out of each one. "I got root beer."

"Great." Marlee set her jacket on the bench seat and grabbed a menu from behind the jars of red pepper flakes and parmesan cheese on the table. She flipped the menu open to the pizza section. "I am *so* hungry."

"Good." Rae tugged the menu down. "I already ordered a large garbage pizza."

"Awesome." Marlee slid the menu back into the holder. "How long ago?"

Rae pointed toward the kitchen. "Long enough that it's almost to our table now."

Marlee glanced over her shoulder and saw Gus himself carrying a large pizza pan in one hand.

"Gus's best for you." The man's thick Greek accent sometimes made it hard to understand him, especially when the place was noisy like tonight. "With everything."

"Anchovies?" Marlee glanced at the pizza then to Rae. "Really?"

Rae shrugged. "I had a craving for them."

Marlee shook her head and smiled at the owner as he slid the pizza pan onto their table. "Thanks, Gus."

The eighty-one-year-old man gave a nod, his craggy face

reminding her of an ancient sea captain's. "Eat." He walked away in an old man's slow gate.

Marlee glanced at Rae to see that she already had a big slice. Marlee took one and slid it onto her plate.

Rae took a big bite and gave a happy sigh. "Gus makes *the best* pizza."

Marlee shook her head. "I must be in the *Twilight Zone*. You never eat garbage pizza, much less anchovies."

Rae grinned as Marlee bit into her own pizza. "That's because I'm pregnant."

Marlee nearly choked on her mouthful. She hurried to chew then swallow. "That's *wonderful*, Rae. Congrats to both you and Bear."

"We suspected it for the past two weeks." Rae practically bounced in her seat. "We just found out for sure from Dr. Martin today. Apparently, that's why I've been having mood swings and want to eat all the time and hungry for weird things. No morning sickness so far. Thank God." She bit into an anchovy on her pizza again.

Marlee felt a bright warmth in her chest at the news. "I'm so excited for you. Have you told your sister?"

Rae shook her head. "I'll tell Carrie when Bear and I visit her and the kids next weekend. I wanted to share the news with her in person."

Marlee sipped her root beer before setting down the red tumbler. "The twins will be beyond excited."

Rae nodded enthusiastically. "The girls will probably think they have a new doll to play with when the baby is born." Rae laughed. "Even though neither of them is into dolls."

"Maybe they'll teach the baby to kick a soccer ball when she or he is bigger." Marlee leaned forward. "Are you going to find out if it's a girl or boy when they can tell?"

"We haven't decided." Rae looked thoughtful. "There's something to say about knowing and being prepared, or just finding out after the birth."

"I'd want to know." Marlee eased back and picked up her slice. "I'd be planning every last moment of it."

Rae laughed. "You would. You always have had to know everything you can about everything that interests you or comes up in your life."

"That's me." Marlee dug into her pizza again.

"Bear and I would like you to be our baby's godmother," Rae said when Marlee set down her pizza.

Marlee wiped her mouth with a napkin and smiled. "Thank you, Rae. I would love to." Marlee laughed. "You know, godmother sounds much too close to grandmother."

Rae grinned. "Grandmotherhood is a long way off for both of us."

"Thank God," Marlee said. "I'm not even ready to be a mom, whenever that might be."

For a few moments they munched on their dinner. When Marlee reached for a second slice, Rae folded her arms on the table. "Have you heard about the small business fundraising event?"

Marlee groaned and looked up at the stained-glass lamp over their table. "I practically committed to Amy Baker this morning that I'd help, before she told me it would be held at Colt's ranch."

"He's really not a bad guy," Rae said tentatively. "Maybe it's time to bury the hatchet."

Marlee sighed and let the thought roll around in her mind. "Maybe."

Rae nodded in the direction of the front door. "Well, here comes your chance."

Marlee wanted to slide down in her seat to hide. She refused to look over her shoulder. "Hell, no."

Rae laughed. "Come on, Marlee. Give it a go."

Two male voices approached from behind Marlee—sounded like Bear and Colt. "You planned this," Marlee hissed.

Rae shook her head. "I knew Bear was stopping by, that's it." Rae straightened and she beamed, positively glowing. "You made it," she said to Bear as he reached the table then slid onto the bench beside her."

Bear kissed her. "Of course."

Marlee felt more than saw the tall, muscular presence beside her. She didn't want to look up, but she made herself do it.

Colt McLeod grinned down at her. "Hey, Marlee."

Marlee sighed and forced a smile. "You might as well have a seat and join us."

"Don't mind if I do." He gave a nod toward the bench seat. "Scoot on over."

Marlee held back another groan. Colt couldn't very well ask Bear to move and sit by his brother. Not to mention each bench only fit two.

She moved as far away as possible, but that was only a few inches. Colt eased in beside her and his big body pressed firmly along her side. Yep, not enough room at this table for the two of them.

Her senses ignited, now on overdrive from his nearness. He smelled so good, of soap and a comforting masculine scent. His body felt warm and hard against hers, and she wondered, not for the first time, what it would be like to be in his arms now that he was a man, as opposed to the lean but muscular teen he had been.

Colt had a larger, more muscular build than his brothers. His biceps bulged beneath his black T-shirt that clung to his perfect torso. His body felt so hard against her as he shifted in his seat. How she longed to see what was under the T-shirt and the denim that molded to his athletic thighs. The man was a work of art.

Marlee's face heated as Colt met her gaze. "How're you doing, sugar?"

She raised her chin. "Save your charm for another woman who will fall for it."

He grinned. "So, I'm charming?"

A flush stole over her. "In your dreams, cowboy."

Colt flashed her a grin. "I've had some pretty good dreams."

Marlee rolled her eyes before turning to Bear. "Congrats, Bear."

He gave his sexy-cute grin. "I can't wait."

"*We* can't wait." Rae rested her head on his shoulder. She looked so happy, so contented, that it made Marlee ache inside. What would it be like to have a love like the two of them shared?

Not something that would come into her life soon, considering she hadn't been on a date in about a hundred years before Ben, she worked at home, and she rarely got out. She had her doubts about Ben. He was a kind of blip on the screen. Yeah, not gonna happen for a loooong time.

"What have you been up to?" Colt had his gaze on her again. He had the most beautiful eyes, the color of whiskey.

She swallowed and tried not to stumble over her words. "Same old, same old."

He raised an eyebrow. "And what would that be, considering I have no idea what's the same with you."

She shrugged. "I edit books all day long, I go for jogs. I crazy quilt. Other than meeting up with friends on occasion, I have about zero excitement in my life."

Colt grinned. "I could cook up some excitement."

She resisted rolling her eyes again. "Oh, *please*. Spare me."

The damned man laughed. "I'll take you dancing. Sounds like you could use a night out."

Her scalp tingled. Was Colt asking her on a date? He was definitely flirting with her.

She was not falling for this. *Again.*

"Thanks, but no thanks."

"Come on, Marlee." The corner of his mouth was turned up in

his sexy-as-hell grin. "We can go to Mickey's Friday night. A live band will be playing."

She narrowed her gaze at him. "What's gotten into you?"

He held her gaze. "I've been wanting to ask you out for the longest time."

She resisted narrowing her eyes and glaring. "I've heard that one before."

Colt sighed. "You're never going to forgive me."

"Nope." She eyed him steadily. "You blew it, and you blew it good."

His expression sobered. "I'm sorry about what happened. I have been since that day—I just never had the chance to tell you."

Marlee's whole body tingled, and she couldn't meet his gaze anymore. She reached for her drink to keep her hands occupied —and her attention away from the man who made her feel like she was on fire and he was the only one who could put it out.

When she had herself under control, the best she could, she met Colt's gaze again. Dang that man for being so sexy and having such beautiful eyes. "You've had plenty of time, Colt. And plenty of opportunity."

This time he looked away. When he had his gaze on her again, he spoke quietly. "I'm a coward. I didn't know how to say it, and it just got harder as time's gone by. You've avoided me, for good reason, and I never took the time I needed to say it. I'm sorry, Marlee. Can we start over?"

She thought about it for a long moment. All the hurt, all the pain. She'd held onto it for so long. Rae was probably right, she should bury the hatchet with Colt. After all, they hadn't been more than teenagers in their senior year.

Marlee took a deep breath before releasing it. "It's a new day. Sure, we can be friends."

He studied her and didn't smile. "How about Mickey's Friday?"

Too soon, too fast.

She paused before giving a slow shake of her head. "No, I don't think so."

"All right." He gave a lopsided smile that she found incredibly endearing. "Doesn't mean I'll give up."

She couldn't help a smile. "Doesn't mean I'll ever say yes."

Bear and Colt joined in eating the huge pizza. As they enjoyed dinner, Marlee could barely breathe from Colt's nearness. She was grateful Colt kept to safe topics, like the latest happenings around town and what he had going on around his ranch.

When they'd polished off the pizza, she'd reached the bottom of her glass of root beer, and he'd finished his beer, Colt asked, "How'd you get here?"

She shrugged. "On my own two feet. I live a fifteen-minute walk from here."

"Well, it's a five-minute drive, so I'll take you home." He straightened. "Can't have you walking home when you're intoxicated."

She snorted back a laugh. "You know perfectly well that I haven't had anything stronger than root beer."

"I only hear the word 'beer.'" His smile turned into a grin and he slid out of the booth and stood. He absolutely towered over her, a good six-three. He braced his hand on the back of the bench seat and looked at Bear and Rae, who'd been talking.

"Marlee walked here, so I'm driving her home."

Marlee's jaw dropped. She started to argue, but Bear and Rae nodded and smiled.

Bear grinned. "See you two soon."

Marlee gripped her jacket in her fist, feeling like she couldn't decline. Colt had put her in a spot in front of Rae and her husband.

Colt stepped back as Marlee held her jacket to her, scooted out of the booth, and got to her feet. She did her best not to glare at Colt.

"Call me tomorrow." Rae had a knowing glint in her eyes.

Marlee gave a little wave and left, not caring if Colt was behind her. Naturally, he was. She could feel his body heat as he came up beside her. He touched his hand to the small of her back and she stiffened as they made their way through the crowd that had grown since she'd arrived.

When they were finally outside, she whirled on him. "You made it too awkward to tell you where to shove your offer of a ride home." She braced her hands on her hips. "Well, let me tell you, Colt McLeod—"

He grasped her by her upper arms, dragged her to him, and cut her off when he pressed his mouth to hers.

CHAPTER 2

Marlee sucked in her breath, completely stunned and unable to think straight as his mouth moved over hers. She placed her palms against his chest, her head suddenly fuzzy while her body burned with fire. Maybe Gus *had* put something in the root beer.

But no, it was totally and completely Colt McLeod who chased words from her mind. She went from trying to push him away to fisting her hands in his T-shirt, gripping him tightly.

Something twisted inside her, and she barely reined herself in as she slowly responded. An almost animal part of her wanted to kiss him with the kind of ferocity that would only get her in trouble.

His mouth was hot as she tasted him, and she found she couldn't get enough. He kissed her long and hard, and she wanted more and more and more.

And then she was gasping for air in the cold, clear night as he drew away and stared down at her. "Let's go, Marlee. I'll drive you home."

Her mind couldn't move past the kiss. She had a hard time

thinking as he guided her toward his big black truck. He helped her into the passenger seat before climbing into the driver's side.

She remained silent as he started the truck. Once they were on the road and her mind had cleared, she finally said, "Why did you do that?"

He flashed her an innocent look. "Do what?"

"Colt." She wanted to smile, but she was too confused. "Why did you kiss me?"

He stared at the road before looking at her. "Because I've wanted to for a long time. A real long time."

She had to think about that for a moment that stretched out, yet nothing was computing. "We've barely spoken over these past years and then tonight you're apologizing, asking me on a date, and kissing me?"

He glanced at her. "We haven't spoken because you avoid me."

"Like the plague." Her words caused him to smile. "I'm not like that," she went on. "I can't feel one way for all this time then flip a switch and suddenly feel another way."

"Can't or won't?" He focused on the road. "I'm thinking it's the latter."

She considered his words. "Maybe." She glanced out the passenger window to watch as he guided his truck into her neighborhood. "I don't know."

Within a few moments, he'd pulled into her driveway and parked.

She frowned and looked at him. "How do you know where I live?"

He shrugged. "You may have pushed me out of your life, but that doesn't mean I don't pay attention."

She stared at him, exasperated. "That makes about zero sense."

He grinned. "Bear told me."

"House number even?" She couldn't believe the man.

"Yep." Colt climbed out the driver's side, not giving her time to respond. He had reached her door before she'd had a chance to find the door release.

He helped her out of the truck and pressed his fingers against her back as he walked with her up the porch steps. She shivered from his touch even though her jacket was between them.

When they reached the door, she dug her key out of her pocket and unlocked her door. She tilted her head and met his gaze. He looked so damned sexy beneath his Stetson. She could just imagine him in nothing but that cowboy hat—

She swallowed, hard. "Thanks for the ride home. I think."

He smiled and her belly fluttered. He cupped her face in his large hands. She couldn't move before he brushed his lips over hers.

The man kept taking her breath away.

He released her and stepped back. "I'll pick you up at seven Friday night."

"What?" She still hadn't gained control of her brain. "No. Wait—"

But he was down the steps and headed out the gate before she could complete her thought. She bit her lower lip as he climbed into his truck and started it. He waited for her to safely go into her home and shut the door behind her. The sound of the truck's big motor filled the night as he drove away.

Marlee held her hand to her heart, and it thudded beneath her palm. What had just happened? Wasn't it only this morning that she had been trying to think of a way to get out of going to Colt's ranch for the event—then Colt kissed her only hours later, and she had let him. Not only had she let him kiss her, but she had been a willing participant.

What the hell?

In a daze she made her way into her kitchen and got a bottle of water out of the fridge. She stared at the clock, surprised to see it was only a bit after eight. Less than forty-eight hours from now, Colt expected to pick her up and go dancing at Mickey's.

She sank into a kitchen chair. Should she? What did she *really* want? If ever there was a time to be honest with herself, this had to be it. She put her head on her arms on the table and squeezed her eyes shut.

Colt's face filled her mind, and she relived the moment when he had pulled her to him and kissed her so fiercely. Her body tingled from head to toe.

Being a seventeen-year-old and hating Colt was one thing—being her age now and holding a grudge was another. Yeah, maybe she should give the grown man the chance she'd refused to give the eighteen-year-old he'd once been. She probably should have forgiven him long ago, and maybe she had. Maybe her grudge was just a habit now, not how she really felt.

He'd been a young man, no more than a kid, when Marlee found out he'd messed around with Sally Farmer. She hadn't believed it when her friends told her, until she caught Colt kissing Sally.

She'd been so hurt. She'd thought she was in love with Colt, and she'd been devasted when he'd thrown that away.

"He was a really dumb teenager." She frowned. "And we were both too young to even think about a long-term relationship. At the time, it was for the best."

She let those thoughts swirl in her mind for a few moments. Colt was a grown man now, mature enough to have a prosperous business and a good reputation in the community. Although, she had heard he was the biggest flirt in the county.

Could it be good between them?

Was she overthinking this? Yeah, she was. Maybe she could get to know the adult Colt and just take it a day at a time.

Marlee straightened in her chair. "All right. Here goes." She allowed herself to think about the incredible kiss and a delicious shiver traveled through her.

Yes, she was finally being honest with herself—she was definitely looking forward to Friday night.

COLT WOKE up the next morning with more energy than he'd felt in ages. He'd dreamt of Marlee, and not for the first time. Only last night at Gus's he'd gotten a lot closer to the real Marlee than he'd figured he could get to her during his waking hours, maybe ever.

Yeah, he'd pushed her, but he didn't know how else to get her attention. He'd gotten her attention, all right. Hopefully he could keep it.

And that kiss had about knocked his boots off. Her beauty always made his gut tighten. From the moment he set eyes on her in the pizza joint, he'd wanted to cart her off and kiss her good and long. The kiss had been better than good, but definitely not long enough to suit him. Hell, it was a start. Just the beginning.

Even when they were teenagers, Colt had thought Marlee was drop-dead gorgeous. The woman she had grown into was even more beautiful. All that glorious chestnut brown hair—last night she'd had it up in a ponytail, and he'd really wanted to let it all down. Her eyes, the achingly blue color of a clear desert sky, had just about undone him.

Funny thing was, he never had a problem approaching women, charming them even. His brother, Bear, had always wondered how it had been so easy for Colt. Maybe too easy, and he'd ended up getting lazy about finding the right woman.

It had taken him years to get around to asking Marlee out. Life had gotten away from him and he'd flirted with and dated plenty of women. But he'd never quite gotten over the one who got away.

Marlee stayed on his mind as he went about chores around the ranch, his dog, Ranger, at his heels. Cattle lowed in the background as Colt hummed a country tune while feeding the horses, and his stable hand mucked out the stalls. His foreman for the Bar-M, Jim, had the day-to-day operation of the ranch and the activities of the cowhands under control as usual. The older man was damned good at his job and Colt was lucky to have him.

Would Marlee be planning to go tomorrow night when Colt stopped by her home to pick her up? The way she'd responded to his kiss last night, he had a good feeling that she'd be ready. A woman didn't kiss a man back like that if she wasn't interested, unless she was faking it. Last thing Marlee Fox would ever do, was fake anything—he'd bet his best horse, Rocky, on it. And he loved that damned horse.

Rocky put his head over the stall door and whickered, as if responding to Colt's thoughts.

"Don't worry, boy." Colt moved to the stall and rubbed the stallion's nose. "I'd never make a bet I didn't think I'd win when it comes to you."

Rocky blew air from his nostrils and snorted.

Colt grinned and patted the horse's neck. "I'll take you up to the canyon tomorrow. How's that sound to you?"

Rocky tossed his head, as if in agreement. The horse was smart as hell—for all Colt knew, the horse *could* understand every word.

Colt patted Rocky one more time. "Go on out to the pasture. It's one hell of a beautiful day."

Rocky snorted again before turning around and heading out.

Colt looked down at Ranger. The Border Collie parked his butt at Colt's feet, and he scratched the blue merle behind his ears. "You bet you're included on the ride."

Rocky barked once, an excited spark to his intelligent eyes.

Colt's phone rang and he pulled it from the holster at his side. He didn't recognize the number, so answered with, "This is Colt McLeod."

"Hi, Colt." A breathless female voice that sounded vaguely familiar filled his ear. "I've missed you."

Colt frowned. "Who is this?"

A pause. "I can't believe you'd forget me." Now the woman

sounded like she was pouting. "This is Sally Farmer. I'm back in town."

Colt nearly groaned. The last person on earth he wanted to talk with was Sally Farmer.

He blew out a breath. "What can I do for you, Sally?"

Another pause, then her voice had an edge to it as if she was angry. "I don't need you to do anything for me." A hesitation, and now she sounded sweet enough to give someone a sugar high. "Let's get together, Colt. How about meeting me at Mickey's for a drink tomorrow night?"

Colt pinched the bridge of his nose with his thumb and forefinger. "I have plans, Sally."

"Are you seeing someone?" Her tone went from syrupy to sharp as a knife.

Her mood change was like watching a heart monitor. Up, down. Up, down.

He wanted to say, *That's none of your business,* but he tried to never be rude to women. After what Sally had done in high school, he had a hard time feeling charitable. But of course, that was a long time ago, just like what he and Marlee were just now going through.

"I am seeing someone," he said.

Dead silence.

"I've got to get back to work, Sally." Colt tipped his head to look at the deep blue sky. "Hope you have a nice time while you're back in town."

Nothing. He looked at the phone to see she'd disconnected the call.

Colt blew out a long breath, then pushed Sally out of his mind. He didn't need her back in his life again.

The sound of a vehicle approaching on the dirt road caught Colt's attention, a welcome reprieve from his thoughts. He walked outside the barn and focused on the road leading from the highway to his ranch. Dust boiled up behind a silver truck—Brady's.

Ranger's ears remained perked as he stood at Colt's side and stared at the oncoming vehicle. The truck's tires thrummed over the cattle guard as it passed beneath the Bar-M sign.

Colt hooked his thumbs in the front pockets of his Wranglers as Brady parked. His younger brother hopped out of the truck and strode around the front.

Ranger trotted over to Brady and wiggled in excitement as Brady reached down to scratch behind his ears. "Good to see you, boy."

Ranger gave one of his happy barks he reserved for family and close friends of Colt's.

"How's it going, bro?" Colt asked in way of greeting.

Brady shrugged as he sauntered over to Colt. "It's goin'."

Colt eyed his brother. "Something's bothering you."

Brady pushed his fingers through his wavy dark hair and turned his attention on the cattle that stirred in the corral. He brought his gaze back to Colt. "Sarah dumped me. She dumped me good."

"Sorry to hear that." Colt braced his hand on Brady's shoulder. "Why don't you come on into the house and you can tell me about it over a beer? It's life's cure-all."

Brady's mouth curved into a slight grin. "I could sure use a good cure."

The two of them walked to the back door of the house and entered through the kitchen. Colt took off his Stetson and tossed it onto the hat tree. Brady added his to the tree that had six other western hats already on it, both felt and straw. Colt liked to have a few to choose from. He wondered if he was like some women he'd heard about and their collection of shoes—only he liked Stetsons and Resistols, and not some fancy-named designer high heels. But then he had maybe ten western hats, not hundreds.

Colt reached into his fridge and snagged a couple of Oak

Creek beers made at a small brewery outside Sedona and grabbed a church key. He popped the cap off one and handed it to Brady, then uncapped his own. He left the opener on the granite countertop and nodded in the direction of his man cave. "We can turn on the game."

"Arizona is playing Dallas today," Brady said as they walked into Colt's favorite space. "Should be a good game."

Colt picked up the remote and threw himself into his ancient recliner. His sister-in-law, Kit, had told him it didn't fit in his sprawling new home, but Colt didn't care. This was the most comfortable piece of furniture he'd ever owned.

He turned on the pregame show, hit mute, then swiveled his recliner toward his brother. Brady had taken the couch and had his boots propped up on a leather ottoman. Colt didn't know whether his brother just wanted to hang out or talk it out.

"Wanna tell me about it?" Colt asked.

Brady took a long pull on his beer then rested the bottle on his thigh. "I think she met another man. Usual BS about it being her fault, it's not me it's her, that kind of crap." Brady shook his head. "I've had a feeling for a while that something was off. I just wasn't sure."

"Tough, bro." Cody scraped at the beer bottle label with his thumbnail.

"Maybe." Brady looked thoughtful. "Hurts like hell after three years, but maybe it's for the best." He rubbed his eyes with his thumb and forefinger before lowering his hand. "It's just after all she and I have been through—hell, I don't know what to think."

"It's better to find out now while you're dating rather than after you've been married for a couple of years." Colt managed a wry smile. "Says the man who was dumped several months ago by a woman who went off with a city slicker."

"That hurts." Brady's expression filled with humor. "Can't get much lower."

Colt laughed. "It worked out. Better him than me."

"True." Brady gave Colt his little-brother mischievous grin. "I hear you took Marlee Fox home last night."

Colt laughed. "Bear been telling stories again?"

Brady shook his head. "Rae. I think she'd like to see you and Marlee together."

"Good to hear. I can use all the help I can get." Colt couldn't help a big grin. "I'm taking Marlee to Mickey's tomorrow night for dancing."

"Way to go." Brady held up his beer in a supportive salute. "I think you finally picked a good one."

"You've got that right." Colt raised his bottle in return as he thought, *Now I've just got to get her and keep her.*

Brady knocked back the rest of his beer and lowered the bottle. "You're never been much for settling down, Colt. I think Marlee's the marrying kind."

Colt held back a frown that wanted to creep in. He hadn't gotten as far as thinking about marriage.

"I kinda figured I'd be the one McLeod who never married." Colt tapped his forefinger on the bottle. "Not sure any woman could change that."

Brady shrugged. "Just sayin'."

Colt would have to think on that. But first things first—he'd enjoy his date with Marlee and see what happened next.

He thought about his big house that was less than a year old. Sometimes it seemed so empty, and he wondered what it would be like with a woman's touch. Now he thought about Marlee in it and could imagine her laughter filling up the empty spaces, her smile brightening everything.

The beer tasted damned good as he took a swig and tried to push aside thoughts of long-term commitments. He didn't have a good track record. He was usually the one to end a relationship, but Alice had broken that streak. Sure hadn't seen that one coming.

Brady brought Colt out of his thoughts. "So, Marlee forgave you for what happened back in high school?"

Colt grimaced. "Not so sure about that. It was a long time ago and I was young and stupid. But honestly, I don't know how what happened did happen. One moment Sally and I were talking, and the next her mouth was on mine."

Brady shook his head. "Have to agree with stupid. You screwed up. You had it good when you two were together."

"Kick a man while he's town." Colt blew out his breath. "But that was a long time ago."

"Sally Farmer moved away, straight out of high school, didn't she?" Brady asked.

Colt gave a nod. "As a coincidence, she called me out of the blue right before you got here."

Brady's brows shot up. "No kidding?"

Colt tried to blow it off. "Said she just got back in town. Wanted me to go with her to Mickey's tomorrow night."

Brady whistled through his teeth. "Talk about timing." He looked at his empty bottle. "Got anymore of these Oak Creeks?"

"I've got plenty of beer." Colt got to his feet and walked back to the kitchen.

Brady got up with him. "When was the last time you saw Sally?"

"Haven't seen her since her parents moved them, who knows where," Colt said. "To tell the truth, after Marlee caught us, Sally and I didn't have much to do with each other. Well, it was more I wouldn't have anything to do with her."

"Sally wanted a relationship?" Brady asked.

"She followed me around the school, left gifts for me on my seat in class, and called me every day after school." Colt grimaced as he thought about those days. "She started showing up at places I would go to in town, and even came out to Mom and Dad's ranch."

"I remember that now." Brady cocked his head to the side. "How'd you get her to stop?"

"She didn't, not until her parents moved and took her with them." Colt grabbed another couple of beers from the fridge. "I'd never been so relieved."

Brady took the beer Colt offered, and they popped off the caps. Brady raised his bottle. "To good days and brotherhood."

Colt clinked his bottle with Brady's. "To being brothers."

They made their way back to the TV room and watched the game. Nothing like a cold beer and a good game of football.

READ MORE OF *Country Rain*!

ALSO BY CHEYENNE MCCRAY

(in reading order)

~Contemporary Cowboys~

"King Creek Cowboys" Series
The McLeods

Country Heat

Country Thunder

Country Storm

Country Rain

Country Monsoon

Country Mist

Country Lightning

Country Frost (coming winter 2024)

"Riding Tall 2" Series
The McBrides Too

Amazed by You

Loved by You

Midnight With You

Wild for You

Sold on You

"Riding Tall" Series

The McBrides

Branded For You

Roping Your Heart

Fencing You In

Tying You Down

Playing With You

Crazy For You

Hot For You

Made For You

Held By You

Belong To You

"Rough and Ready" Series

The Camerons

Silk and Spurs

Lace and Lassos

Champagne and Chaps

Satin and Saddles

Roses and Rodeo (with Creed McBride from **"Riding Tall" Series**)

Roses and Rodeo (with Creed McBride)

Lingerie and Lariats

Lipstick and Leather

~Romantic Suspense~

"Sworn to Protect Series"

Exposed Target

Shadow Target coming 2024

Lethal Target coming 2025

Moving Target coming 2025

"Deadly Intent" Series

Hidden Prey

No Mercy

Taking Fire

Point Blank

Chosen Prey

"Armed and Dangerous" Series

Zack

Luke

Clay

Kade

Alex (a novella)

Eric (a novella)

"Recovery Enforcement Division" Series

Ruthless

Fractured

Vendetta

Save by purchasing Boxed Sets

Riding Tall 2 Box Set Volume One

Amazed by You

Loved by You

Midnight with You

Riding Tall 2 Box Set Volume Two

Wild for You

Sold on You

Riding Tall the First Boxed Set

Includes

Branded for You

Roping Your Heart

Fencing You In

Riding Tall the Second Boxed Set

Includes

Tying You Down

Playing with You

Crazy for You

Riding Tall the Third Boxed Set

Includes

Hot for You

Made for You

Held by You

Belong to You

Rough and Ready Boxed Set One

Includes

Silk and Spurs

Lace and Lassos

Champagne and Chaps

Rough and Ready Boxed Set Two

Includes

Satin and Saddles

Roses and Rodeo

Lingerie and Lariats

Armed and Dangerous Box Set One

Includes

Zack

Luke

Clay

Armed and Dangerous Box Set Two

Kade

Alex

Eric

~Romantic Suspense~

Deadly Intent Box Set 1

Hidden Prey

No Mercy

Taking Fire

Deadly Intent Box Set 2

Point Blank

Chosen Prey

Recovery Enforcement Division: the Collection

Ruthless

Fractured

Vendetta

~Paranormal Romance~

"Dark Sorcery" Series

The Forbidden

The Seduced

The Wicked

The Enchanted (novella)

The Shadows

The Dark

Cheyenne Writing as Debbie Ries

∞

~Shawna Taylor Cozy Mysteries~

Cooking up Murder

Recipe for Killing

Pinch of Peril

Delicious Death

Taste of Danger

ABOUT CHEYENNE

Cheyenne McCray is an award-winning, *New York Times* and *USA Today* best-selling author who grew up on a ranch in southeastern Arizona and has written over one hundred published novels and novellas. Chey also writes cozy mysteries as **Debbie Ries**. She enjoys creating stories of suspense, love, and redemption with characters and worlds her readers can get lost in.

Chey and her husband live with their two Ragdoll cats, two corgis, and two poodle-mixes in southeastern Arizona. She enjoys going on long walks, traveling around the world, and searching for her next adventure and new ideas, as well as building miniature houses, quilting, and listening to audiobooks.

Find out more about Chey, how to contact her, and her books at **https://cheyennemccray.com.**

~

Sign up for Cheyenne's Newsletter
to keep up with Chey and her latest novels
http://cheyennemccray.com/newsletter

Made in United States
Troutdale, OR
07/25/2024